La Vendée
Volume II

by

Anthony Trollope

Double 9 BOOKS

La Vendée
Volume II
by Anthony Trollope

ISBN: 978-93-68095-72-9

Published by

DOUBLE 9 BOOKS
2/13-B, Ansari Road
Daryaganj, New Delhi – 110002
info@double9books.com
www.double9books.com
Tel. 011-40042856

ABOUT THE AUTHOR

Renowned for his Chronicles of Barsetshire series and the Palliser novels, Anthony Trollope was a prolific and renowned English novelist. Trollope was born into a middle-class household, but his early years were characterized by chaotic family dynamics and financial hardships. In spite of these obstacles, he succeeded in his career as a civil servant in the British Post Office, where he spent more than thirty years. Published in 1847, Trollope's debut book, "The Macdermots of Ballycloran," marked the beginning of his writing career. He proceeded to produce travelogues, non-fiction books, short stories, and 47 novels during his lifetime. The richly detailed portrayal of Victorian life, the astute observation of human nature, and the examination of contemporary moral and social issues define Trollope's writing. His books frequently include nuanced individuals battling social and personal issues against the backdrop of small-town England or the corridors of political power. Trollope is regarded as one of the greatest Victorian novels because of his realistic depiction of ordinary life, complex narratives, and witty writing.

CONTENTS

CHAPTER I
SAUMUR

In the next three days the Vendeans bombarded the town, and during that time fired against it everything they could cram into their cannons, in the shape of warlike missiles; and they did not do so in vain, for the walls, in portions, began to give way and to crumble into the moat, which ran round the town, and communicated with the river Loire on each side of it. The town is built on the Loire, and between the Loire and the Thoué. After passing over the latter river at the bridge of Fouchard, the road in a few yards came to the draw-bridge over the moat; and from the close vicinity of the two rivers, no difficulty was found in keeping the moat supplied with water in the driest weather. About a mile below the town, the Thoue runs into the Loire.

Cathelineau found the men very impatient during the bombardment; they did not now dream of going home till the work was over, and Saumur taken; but they were very anxious to make a dash at the walls of the town; they could not understand why they should not clamber into the citadel, as they had done, over the green sods into the camp at Varin. On the fourth morning they were destined to have their wish. A temporary bridge over the Thoué had been made near Varin, over which a great portion of the cannon had been taken to a point near the Loire, from which the royalists had been able to do great damage to the walls; they had succeeded in making a complete breach of some yards, through which an easy entrance might be made, were it not for the moat; much of the rubbish from the walls had fallen into it, so as considerably to lessen the breadth; but there was still about twenty feet of water to be passed, and it was impossible, under the immediate guns of the castle, to contrive anything in the shape of a bridge.

Notwithstanding the difficulties of the place, it was decided that Larochejaquelin should take two hundred of his men and endeavour to make his way through the water, and while he was doing this, de Lescure was to force his passage over the bridge at Fouchard, and if possible, carry the gate of the town; in doing this he would pass under the heights of Bournan, and to this point M. d'Elbée was to accompany him with the great bulk of the army, so as to secure his flank from any attack from the republican force, which still retained their position there, and which had hitherto kept up an intercourse with the town across the bridge of Fouchard.

At five o'clock the greater portion of the army left the camp with d'Elbée and de Lescure. When they came within two furlongs of the bridge, the army separated, the chief body remaining with M. d'Elbée and the remainder going on with M. de Lescure towards the town. The road turns a little before it reaches the bridge over the Thoué, and up to this point, the Vendeans, in their progress, were tolerably protected from the guns of the town; but immediately they turned upon the bridge, they became exposed to a tremendous fire. The men at once perceived this and hesitated to cross the river; two of the foremost of their men fell as they put their feet upon the bridge.

De Lescure had marched from the camp at the head of his men. Father Jerome was on his right hand, and Stofflet and Adolphe Denot at his left. Henri had asked his friend to accompany him in the attack which he was to make near the river, but Adolphe had excused himself, alleging that he had a great dislike to the water, and that he would in preference accompany Charles de Lescure. Henri had not thought much about it, and certainly had imputed no blame to his friend, as there would be full as much scope for gallantry with his cousin as with himself. When de Lescure saw that his men hesitated, he said, "Come my men, forward with 'Marie Jeanne,' we will soon pick their locks for them," and rushed on the bridge alone; seeing that no one followed him he returned, and said to Denot:

"We must shew them an example, Adolphe; we will run to the other side of the bridge and return; after that, they will follow us."

De Lescure did not in the least doubt the courage of his friend, and again ran on to the bridge. Stofflet and Father Jerome immediately followed him, but Adolphe Denot did not stir. He was armed with a heavy sabre, and when de Lescure spoke to him, he raised his arm as though attempting to follow him, but the effort was too much for him, his whole body shook, his face turned crimson, and he remained standing where he was. As soon as de Lescure found that Adolphe did not follow him, he immediately came back, and taking him by the arm, shook him slightly, and whispered in his ear:

"Adolphe, what ails you? remember yourself, this is not the time to be asleep," but still Denot did not follow him; he again raised his arm, he put out his foot to spring forward, but he found he could not do it; he slunk back, and leant against the wall at the corner of the bridge, as though he were fainting.

De Lescure could not wait a moment longer. He would have risked anything but his own reputation to save that of his friend; but his brave companions were still on the bridge, and there he returned for the third time; his cap was shot away, his boot was cut, his clothes were pierced in different places, but still he was not himself wounded.

"See, my friends," said he aloud to the men behind him, "the blues do not know how to fire," and he pointed to his shoulder, from which, as he spoke, a ball had cut the epaulette.

He then crossed completely over the bridge, together with Stofflet and the priest; the people with one tremendous rush followed him, and Adolphe Denot was carried along with the crowd.

As soon as they found themselves immediately beneath the walls of the town, they were not exposed to so murderous a fire as they had been on the bridge itself, but still the work was hot enough. 'Marie Jeanne' had been carried across with them, and was soon brought into play; they had still enough ammunition left to enable their favourite to show her puissance in battering against the chief gates of Saumur. The men made various attempts to get into the town, but they were not successful, though the gates were shattered to pieces, and the passage was almost free; the republican troops within were too strong, and their firing too hot. At last the blues made a sortie from the town, and drove the Vendeans back towards the bridge; M. de Lescure still kept his place in the front, and was endeavouring to encourage his men to recover their position, when a ball struck his arm and broke it, and he fell with his knee upon the ground. As soon as the peasants saw him fall, and found that he was wounded, they wanted to take him in their arms, and carry him at once back across the bridge, but he would not allow them.

"What ails you, friends?" said he; "did you never never see a man stumble before? Come, the passage is free; now at length we will quench our thirst in Saumur," and taking his sword in his left hand, he again attempted to make good his ground.

M. d'Elbée had seen the Vendeans retreating back towards the bridge, and knowing that victory with them must be now or never (for it would have been impossible to have induced the peasants to remain longer from their homes, had they been repulsed), he determined to quit his post and to second de Lescure at the bridge. The firing from the town had ceased, for the republicans and royalists were so mixed together, that the men on the walls would have been as likely to kill their friends as their enemies; and as the first company, fatigued, discouraged and overpowered, were beginning to give way, d'Elbée, with about two thousand men, pushed across the bridge, and the whole mass of the contending forces, blues and Vendeans together, were hurried back through the gateway into the town; and de Lescure, as he entered it, found that it was already in the hands of his own party—the white flag was at that moment rising above the tricolour on the ramparts.

Adolphe Denot was one of the first of the Vendeans who entered the town through the gate. This shewed no great merit in him, for, as has been said, the men who had made the first attack, and the republicans who opposed it, were carried into the town by the impulse of the men behind them; but still he had endeavoured to do what he could to efface the ineffable disgrace which he felt must now attach to him in the opinion of M. de Lescure. As they were making their way up the principal street, still striking down the republicans wherever they continued to make resistance, but more often giving quarter, and promising protection, de Lescure with a pistol held by the barrel in his left hand, and with his right arm hastily tied up in the red handkerchief taken from a peasant's neck, said to the man who was next to him, but whom he did not at the moment perceive to be Denot:

"Look at Larochejaquelin, the gallant fellow; look at the red scarf on the castle wall. I could swear to him among a thousand."

"Yes," said Adolphe, unwilling not to reply when spoken to, and yet ashamed to speak to de Lescure, "yes, that is Henri. I wish I were with him."

"Oh, that is you, is it?" said de Lescure, just turning to look at him, and then hurrying away. But before he had moved on five paces, he returned, and putting his pistol into his girdle, gave Adolphe his left hand, and whispered to him:

"No one shall ever hear of it, Adolphe," said he, "and I will forget it. Think of your Saviour in such moments, Adolphe, and your heart will not fail you again."

The tears came into Denot's eyes as de Lescure left him. He felt that he must be despised; he felt grateful for the promise which had been given him, and yet he felt a kind of hatred for the man to whom he had afforded an opportunity of forgiving him. He felt that he never could like de Lescure again, never be happy in his company; he knew that de Lescure would religiously keep his word, that he would never mention to human being that horrid passage at the bridge; but he knew also that it could never be forgotten. Adolphe Denot was not absolutely a coward; he had not bragged that he would do anything which he knew it was contrary to his nature to do, when he told Agatha that he would be the first to place the white flag on the citadel of Saumur: he felt then all the aspirations of a brave man; he felt a desire even to hurry into the thick of the battle; but he had not the assured, sustained courage to support him in the moment of extreme danger. As de Lescure said, his heart failed him.

We must now return to Henri Larochejaquelin. He had taken with him two hundred of the best men from the parishes of St. Aubin, St. Laud and Echanbroignes; four or five officers accompanied him, among whom was a young lad, just fourteen years of age; his name was Arthur Mondyon, and he was a cadet from a noble family in Poitou; in the army he had at first been always called Le Petit Chevalier. His family had all emigrated, and he had been left at school in Paris; but on the breaking out of the wars he had run away from school, had forged himself a false passport into La Vendée, and declared his determination of fighting for his King. De Lescure had tried much to persuade him to stay at Clisson, but in vain; he had afterwards been attached to a garrison that was kept in the town of Chatillon, as he would then be in comparative safety; but the little Chevalier had a will of his own; he would not remain within walls while fighting was going on, and he had insisted on accompanying Larochejaquelin to Saumur. He was now installed as Henri's aide-de-camp.

Jacques Chapeau also accompanied the party who were to make their way into the town through the water. The men were all armed with muskets and bayonets, but their muskets were not loaded, nor did they carry any powder with them; it would have been useless in the attack they were about to make, and was much wanted elsewhere.

Henri was at his post about the time at which de Lescure was preparing to cross the bridge at Fouchard. It was an awful looking place at which ha had to make his entrance there was certainly a considerable breach in the wall, and the fragments of it had fallen into the fosse, so as to lessen its width; but, nevertheless, there was full twenty feet of running water to cross, which had more the appearance of a branch of the river Loire, than of a moat round a town.

Henri saw that his men looked a little alarmed at what they had to go through; he had a light straw hat on his head, and taking it off, he threw it into the water, a little above the point he had to pass, and as the running water carried it down he said:

"Whoever gives me that on the other side will be my friend for life." And as he spoke he himself leapt into the water, and swam across.

Jacques made a plunge for the hat: had it been in the middle of the Loire he would have gone after it under similar circumstances, though he couldn't swim a stroke; he did not go near the hat however, but went head over heels into the water; the impetus carried him through, and he was the second to scramble upon the broken mortar on the other side. The Chevalier was more active; he leapt in and seized the hat as it was going down the stream, and swimming like a young duck, brought it back to its owner.

"Ah! Chevalier," said Henri, reproaching him playfully, and helping him up out of the water, "you have robbed some poor fellow of a chance; you, you know, cannot be more my friend, than you already are."

The men quickly followed: they all got a ducking; some few lost their arms, one or two were slightly wounded by their comrades, but none of them were drowned. Henri soon made his way over the ruins into the town, and carried everything before him. The greater part of the garrison of the town were endeavouring to repulse the attack made by de Lescure; others had retired into the castle, in which the republican General thought that he might still hold out against the Vendeans. Many were already escaping out of the town by the bridge over the Loire, and throwing down their arms, were hurrying along the road to Tours.

It was in this manner, and almost without opposition, that Larochejaquelin found himself, together with his brave followers, in the middle of Saumur; their own success astonished them; hardly a shot was fired at them in their passage; they went through the town without losing a man; the republican soldiers whom they did see threw down their arms and fled; the very sight of the Vendeans in the centre of the town overwhelmed them with panic. The appearance of Henri's troop was very singular; every man wore round his neck and round his waist a red cotton handkerchief; this costume had been adopted to preserve Larochejaquelin from the especial danger of being made the butt of republican marksmen. There was now no especial mouchoir rouge among them. They certainly had a frightful appearance, as they hurried through the streets with their bayonets fixed, dripping with mud and water, and conspicuous with their red necks and red waists; at least so thought the republicans, for they offered very little opposition to them.

Henri had just time to see that his friends had entered the town by the gate on the Doué road, but he did not wait to speak to them. The republican soldiers were escaping from the town in the opposite direction, and he could not resist the temptation of following them. He was at the head of his men, just passing over the Loire by a wooden bridge, called the bridge of the Green Cross, and having possessed himself of a sword in his passage through the town, was making good use of it, when a dragoon turned suddenly round, and fired a pistol almost in his face: near as the man was to him, in his hurry he missed him, and the bullet merely grazed Henri's cheek, without even raising the skin. "Ah, bungler," said Henri, raising his sword, "you are no good for either King or nation," and he struck the unfortunate man dead at his feet.

Not only the soldiers, but the inhabitants of the town were escaping by hundreds over the bridge, and Henri saw that if he pursued them farther, he must, sooner or later, find himself surrounded and overpowered by numbers; he returned, therefore, and destroyed the bridge, so as to prevent the return of the soldiers who had fled in their first panic, and also to prevent any more of the inhabitants from leaving their homes.

"God has certainly fought on our side today," said he to one of his Mends: "with barely two hundred men, all dripping like drowned rats, we have made our way, almost without opposition, through the town, and thousands of soldiers are even yet flying before us."

"Ah! M. Henri," said the little Chevalier, "it is a great honour to fight for one's King; one fears nothing then: a single royalist should always drive before him ten republicans."

Henri now returned and joined de Lescure, who was in possession of the town, though the citadel was still in the hands of General Quetineau, who held the command of the garrison. It was not till the cousins had embraced each other, that Henri saw that de Lescure was wounded.

"Yes," said de Lescure, "I have at length acquired the privilege of shedding my blood in the cause; but it is only a broken arm; Victorine will have a little trouble with me when I return to Clisson."

"And Adolphe, my brave Adolphe, you are wounded, too?" said Henri.

Denot muttered something, and turned away; he did not dare to look his friends in the face.

"He envies me my honour," said de Lescure; "but it might have been his chance as well as mine, for he was not two feet from me when I was wounded." This was true, for de Lescure had been struck after Denot had crossed the bridge with the other men.

A flag of truce was now sent out by General Quetineau to the royalists, with a proposal that he would give up the castle, and lay down his arms, on being allowed to march out with all his men, and take the road to Angers; but this proposition was not acceded to.

"No!" said de Lescure to the General's messenger: "tell M. Quetineau that the Vendeans cannot accede to those terms—we cannot allow his soldiers to march to Angers, and to return within a week to inflict new cruelties on our poor peasants. M. Quetineau must surrender without any terms: the practices of our army must be his only guarantee, that his men will not be massacred in cold blood, as the unfortunate royalists are massacred when they fall into the hands of the republicans."

The republicans were not in a condition to insist upon anything; as M. de Lescure had said, the practices of the Vendeans were a guarantee that no blood would be unnecessarily shed, and relying on this assurance alone, M. Quetineau surrendered the castle and gave up his sword. De Lescure took possession of it till he should be able to hand it over to his General, and the Vendeans found themselves complete masters of Saumur.

There was, however, still a very strong detachment of republican troops on the heights of Bournan, who were watched on one side by Foret and his detachment, and on the other by a portion of M. d'Elbée's army. These men had done some execution, as they covered with their cannon a portion of the road over which the Vendeans had passed, but they had taken no active part whatever in the engagement. What made this the more singular, was that the garrison at Bournan was composed of the very best soldiers of the French republican army. They were under the command of General Coustard, who kept his position during the whole attack, inactive and unmolested; had he attacked M. d'Elbée's army in the rear, when that officer advanced to support de Lescure's division, the Vendeans would probably have been destroyed between the two republican armies. Whether the two Generals of the Convention misunderstood each other, or whether the soldiers at Bournan were unwilling to rout the royalists, it is impossible to say; but they remained at Bournan till the night, and then leaving their post during the darkness, made good their retreat to Angers.

As soon as the white flag was seen on the walls of Saumur, Cathelineau left the position which he had held, and entered the town. It was greatly in opposition to his own wishes that he had been induced to remain at a distance from the absolute attack, and now he felt almost ashamed of himself as the officers and men crowded round him to congratulate him on the victory which he had gained.

"No, M. de Lescure," he said, as that officer tendered him General Quetineau's sword, "no, I will never take it from him who has won it with so much constancy and valour. I must own I envy you your good fortune, but I will not rob you of the fruits of your exertions."

"But Cathelineau," said the other, "you are our General, the customs of war require—"

"The customs of war are all changed," replied Cathelineau, "when such as you and M. de Larochejaquelin make yourselves second to a poor postillion; at any rate," he added, pressing between his own, the left hand of M. de Lescure, which still held the sword, "if I am to be the commander, I must be obeyed. M. de Lescure will not set a bad example when I tell him to keep General Quetineau's sword."

"And you, General Quetineau," said Cathelineau, "what are your wishes—your own personal wishes I mean? I have not forgotten that you alone of the republican leaders have shewn mercy to the poor royalists, when they were in your power; you at any rate shall not say that the Vendean brigands do not know how to requite kind services." Cathelineau alluded to the name which the republicans had given to the royalists at the commencement of the war.

"It little matters to me," said Quetineau, "what becomes of me; were you to give me unconditional liberty, I should go to Paris—and the Convention would accuse me of betraying my trust, and I should become another victim of the guillotine."

"Of the guillotine!" said Henri; "why, what bloody monsters are those you serve they send you soldiers who know nothing but how to run; do they expect that with such troops as these you should be victorious, when opposed to men who are individually striving for everything that is dear to them?"

"The Convention," said Quetineau, "would ensure success by punishing defeat. You will find in the end that they are politic; there will, however, be many victims, and I am fated to be one of them."

"Stay with us, General Quetineau," said de Lescure, "join our forces, and here you will find that honesty and courage are respected. You cannot, you do not approve of the tyranny of the Convention. We know each other of old, and I know that in joining the army, you never intended to serve under a Republic. You cannot say that in your heart you are a republican."

"Did I wish to shew myself a royalist, it would not now become me to proclaim myself one," answered Quetineau. "I entered the army of the King, but I have chosen to remain a soldier of the Republic. Whatever may be my feelings, adversity shall not make me false to the colours I have carried; besides, gentlemen, if I escaped the anger of the Convention myself, I have a wife in Paris, whose life would be made to satisfy it; under such circumstances, I presume you would not counsel me to become a royalist."

This was an argument which it was impossible to answer. General Quetineau accepted the present of his liberty, and soon as he was free, he returned to Paris; he was immediately sent to the revolutionary tribunal and tried for his life; and as he himself had predicted, was guillotined by the Convention for the cowardice of the troops, whom he had been called upon to take under his command. In the old days of Greece, when the Kings sinned, the people suffered for it: this law was reversed under the first French Republic; when the soldiers ran away, the Generals were beheaded.

The joy of the Vendeans, when they found themselves masters of Saumur, knew no bounds, but they were grotesque rather than unruly in their demonstrations; they plundered nothing from the poor people, or even from the shopkeepers; the money that was found in the republican chest was divided among them, but as this consisted almost entirely of assignats, it was of but little value. The shopkeepers were surprised at the liberality of their enemies and conquerors, who were willing to dispose of these assignats for anything they would fetch—a little wine, or a few ounces of tobacco; whereas, their own friends, the republicans, had insisted that they should be taken at their nominal value as money, for all goods exposed for sale.

An enormous poplar had been planted by the towns-people in the centre of the marketplace, which they called the tree of liberty. This was now a doomed tree. On the evening of the day in which they took the town, the royalist peasants went in procession, and with many cheers hewed it to the ground; it was then treated with every possible contumely—it was chopped, and hacked, and barked; it was kicked, and cuffed, and spat upon; the branches were cut off, and on the bare top was placed a large tattered cap of liberty; the Vendean marksmen then turned out, and fired at the cap till it was cut to pieces; after that, all the papers and books, which had belonged to the municipality, every document which could be found in the Town-hall, were brought into the square, and piled around the roots of the tree; and then the whole was set on fire—and tree, papers, and cap of liberty, were consumed together.

On the next morning, considerable difficulty was experienced in disposing of the prisoners there were about two thousand in the town, and the Vendeans knew that they had no means of keeping them, nor did they wish to be at the great expense of feeding them; it was contrary to their inclination, their practice, and their consciences, to kill them in cold blood: and they knew from experience, that if they gave them their liberty, the same men would return within a fortnight, newly-armed, to carry on the war against their liberators, in spite of any oaths they might take to the contrary.

"I'll tell you what we will do, M. Henri," said Chapeau, speaking to his master, "we will put a mark upon them, so that if we catch them again, we may know them; and then I do think it would be all right to hang them; or perhaps for the second time we might cut off their ears, and hang them the third time."

"But how would you mark them, Jacques; men are not like cattle that you can brand them."

"I will tell you what," said the little Chevalier, "shave them all like pigs; they cannot all buy wigs, and we shall know them by their bald sconces."

"That is the very thing, M. Arthur," said Chapeau delighted, "we will shave their heads as clear as the palm of my hand. I am an excellent barber myself; and I will even get a dozen or two assistants; hair shall be cheap in Saumur tomorrow; though I fear soap and razors will be scarce."

Chapeau was so delighted with the proposal that he at once hurried away to carry it into execution; and Arthur, though he felt that his dignity as an officer would be somewhat compromised, could not resist the boyish temptation to follow him and see the fun.

He and Chapeau were not long in raising an efficient corps of barbers and assistant barbers; and few of the shopkeepers, when called upon, thought it advisable to refuse the loan of a razor and a shaving dish. They established themselves in the large room of the Town-hall, and had the prisoners brought in by a score at a time; vehemently did the men plead for their hair, and loud did they swear that if allowed to escape free, they would never again carry arms against the Vendeans; but neither their oaths or their prayers were of any avail, nor yet the bribes which were offered by those who had ought to give; the order to sit down was given imperatively, and if not immediately obeyed, the command was somewhat roughly enforced.

They were shaved by twenty at a time, and while one lot was being operated on, another twenty, who were next destined to fill the chairs, were kept standing against the wall. The long hair was first cut off with scissors, and then the head and whiskers were closely shaved. The first candidates for the soap-dish were very unruly under the operation, but they only got their ears snipped and their skin chipped, and had to return to their prisons with their polls all bloody as well as bald. Those who looked on, took a lesson from the folly of their comrades, and most of them remained quiet. The manoeuvres of the men however were very different during the process; some took it with good humour, and endeavoured to laugh as their locks were falling; some sat still as death; others looked fierce and warlike; some were even moved to tears; some fought, and kicked and scratched, and at last had to be corded to their seats. One unfortunate went down upon his knees, and implored Chapeau by the memory of his mistress, if ever he had been in love, by his regard for his wife, if he chanced to be married, not to shave his head. He was engaged to be married, he said, to a young girl at Angers, who had many lovers; she had preferred him for the beauty of his hair: if he returned back bald, he knew that he would be rejected. Chapeau for a time was moved, but the patriot and the royalist triumphed over the man, and Jacques, turning away his face on which a tear was gleaming, with a wave of his hand motioned the young man to the chair.

Insult was added to injury, for the Chevalier stood at the door with a brush, and a large jar of red paint, and as each man went out of the room, Arthur made a huge cross upon his bare pate. The poor wretches in their attempt to rub it off, merely converted the cross into a red patch, and as they were made to walk across the market-place with their bald red heads, they gave rise to shouts of laughter, not only from the royalists, but from the inhabitants of the town.

For three days the shaving went on, and as the men became experienced from practice, it was conducted with wonderful rapidity. At last, the prisoners were all deprived of their hair, and set at liberty—a temporary bridge was thrown across the Loire, near the Green Cross, and the men were allowed to march over. As soon as they found themselves on the other side of the Loire, they were free.

"Come, my bald pates, come my knights of the ruddy scalp," said Jacques, standing at the corner of the bridge as they passed over, "away with you to the Convention; and if your friends like your appearance, send them to Saumur, and they shall be shaved close, and the barber shall ask for no fee; but remember, if you return again yourselves, your ears will be the next sacrifice you will be called on to make for your country."

CHAPTER II
COUNCIL OF WAR

The taking of the fortified town of Saumur, and the total dispersion of the large army which had been collected there by the Republic, was an enterprise of much greater magnitude than anything which had previously been undertaken by the Vendeans: it gave them great advantages, it supplied them plentifully with arms, ammunition and clothes for their soldiers, and greatly inspirited the peasants; but it made the Convention feel that it had no contemptible enemy to deal with in La Vendée, and that the best soldiers of France would be required to crush the loyalty which inspired the peasants of Anjou and Poitou.

The Vendean leaders felt that their responsibilities were greatly increased, and that very much depended on the decision to which they might now come as regarded their further operations. A general council of war was accordingly held in Saumur, at which the matter was debated among them. Twelve of the Vendeans were admitted to this consultation, and all others were strictly excluded; they were Cathelineau, Bonchamps, who though badly wounded, had caused himself to be brought thither from Doué, de Lescure, who had remained in action for eight hours after his arm was broken, and had consequently suffered much from it, Larochejaquein, d'Elbée, Stofflet, Adolphe Denot, Father Jerome, Foret, M. Donnessan, Lescure's father-in-law, Marigny, and the Prince de Talmont.

The first question was the selection of a chief officer. Cathelineau had been named before the battle of Saumur; but, as he himself alleged, his command was to last only during that siege; he had been, he said, selected for a special purpose, which purpose, by the grace of God, was accomplished, and he was now ready to resign his commission into the hands of those who had given it to him.

"I am not so foolish," said he, "as to suppose that I am qualified to take the command in the war which we have now to carry on. No; one privilege I beg to exercise on retiring from my command. I will name a successor; let any one who pleases name another; we will then put it to the vote, and let him who has most votes be our General."

"So be it," said Henri. "Nothing can be better."

"I name M. de Lescure," said Cathelineau. "Some of us are beloved by the people, but are not educated; others are highly educated, but are not yet known to the peasants. We are all, I am sure, brave men: but M. de Lescure is beloved by all; his knowledge fits him for his high position, and his cool, constant, determined courage, no man who has seen him in the hour of battle will doubt. I name M. de Lescure."

De Lescure was about to rise, when Henri put his hand upon his friends arm, and said:

"Let me speak, Charles. We all know that what Cathelineau has said of my cousin is no more than the truth. Be still, Charles: when I have spoken you can then say what you please, but I am sure you will agree with me. Nevertheless, I will not give my vote that he be our chief General. Cathelineau has desired that any one differing from him should name another, and that the question should then be put to the vote. I differ from him, and, therefore, I name another. I name the good Cathelineau, the Saint of Anjou."

"Now let us vote," said the Prince de Talmont. "Come, Bonchamps, do you begin."

"I never heard of deposing a Commander-in-Chief in consequence of a complete victory," said Bonchamps. "The Convention murders their Generals when they are defeated, but even the Convention rewards them for victory. I vote for Cathelineau."

"And you, Foret," said the Prince.

"I say Cathelineau," said Foret: "the peasants generally would be disappointed to see any put above him."

"I certainly vote for Cathelineau," said Father Jerome, who came next.

"We should be offending our Creator," said M. d'Elbée, "were we to reject the great and good Commander, whom His gracious providence has sent us. I vote for Cathelineau."

"And you, M. Denot," said the Prince. Adolphe Denot especially disliked Cathelineau: he was jealous of his reputation and popularity: he could not bear to feel himself in any way under the control of a man so much his inferior in rank; he fancied, moreover, that Cathelineau regarded Agatha Larochejaquelin; he had been quick enough to perceive that the ineffable grace and beauty of his mistress had filled the heart of the poor postillion with admiration, and he feared that his own rejection had been caused by some mutual feeling in Agatha's breast, which future events might warm into love. Adolphe, therefore, hated Cathelineau, and would have delighted, had he dared to do so, to express his disapprobation of the choice; but, after pausing for a few moments, he found that he did not dare; so he merely said:

"Oh, Cathelineau, of course. When you are all resolved, what's the use of voting about it?"

"To show that we all are resolved," said de Lescure; "to make Cathelineau understand that it is positively his duty to take the position we wish him to fill."

And so, one after another, they all recorded their votes that Cathelineau should be the Commander-in-Chief of the Vendean army; and they all declared that they would, without reserve, obey any military orders, which he might give them.

"Well, gentlemen," said he, again seating himself at the head of the table, "I should pay but a bad compliment to your understanding, were I any further to insist on my own unworthiness. I will not, at any rate, be wanting in zeal for the good cause, and I will trust to Him who directs us all, for assistance in the difficult duties which you have imposed on me."

They then debated on the all-important question of what should be their next movement, and on this subject there was much difference of opinion. Bonchamps was again asked to speak first, and he advised that they should at once proceed to Paris.

"We can do nothing," said he, "while the present Convention sits in Paris; it has but one head, but it has ten thousand bloody hands. There can be no peace, no rest in France, while Danton, Robespierre and Barrère are omnipotent. Let us at once start for Paris: Brittany will join us, and parts of Normandy; the Southerns will follow us; the men of Bordeaux and of the Gironde: have not their own orators, the leaders of the Revolution, been murdered in their seats, because they were not willing that all France should become one Golgotha? Lyons, even, and Marseilles, are now sick of the monsters who have crawled forth from the haunts of the Jacobins to depopulate the country, and annihilate humanity. There is now but a small faction, even in Paris, to whom the restoration of order would not be acceptable. The intensity of their cruelty is the only strength of the governing faction; the extent of their abominations alone makes them terrible. Hundreds will fly from one Indian snake, so potent is its venom, so sure to inflict death: but let one brave man set his heel upon its head, and the noxious animal is destroyed for ever: so it is with the party who now rules the Convention. Now that we have with us the all-powerful prestige of victory, let us march at once to Paris; hundreds will join us on the way, and what force can at the moment be collected to stop us? Let us proceed at once to Paris, and proclaim at the door of the Convention, in the gardens of the Tuilleries, in the Place Louis Quinze, where our sainted monarch so nobly shed his blood, that France again submits herself to her King."

"Would that we could!" said de Lescure; "would that the spirit of revolution was yet sufficiently quenched in France to allow us to follow your advice; but there is much, very much to be done before a royalist army can march from La Vendée to Paris; unthought of sufferings to be endured, the blood of thousands to be sacrificed, before France will own that she has been wrong in the experiment she has made. We must fight our battles by inches, and be satisfied, if, when dying, we can think that we have left to our children a probability of final victory. Normandy and the Gironde may be unwilling to submit to the Jacobin leaders, but they are as yet as warmly attached to the Republic as Paris itself. And, Bonchamps, you little know the dispositions and character of the men, who at our bidding have left their homes and come to Saumur, if you think that at our bidding they will march to Paris; they are even now burning to return home, to recount to their wives and children what they have done.

"Not half the number that came to Saumur would leave the town with us on the road to Paris; and before we could reach Tours, the army would have melted away from us like snow from a mountain top, when the sun begins to shine. It is here, in our own locality, that we should endeavour to extend our influence. In Southern Brittany the people, I believe, are with us, but the towns are full of the troops of the Republic. Let us drive them out of Angers, Ancenis, and Nantes, as we have driven them from Saumur. Let us force them from the banks of the Loire, and become masters of the coast of Southern Brittany. Then we may expect men and money from England. Then we may fairly hope for such foreign aid as may enable us to face the Republic; but at present, if we march to Paris, we march to certain destruction."

"M. de Lescure is right," said Stofflet, "our men would not go far from their homes; we must remember that they are not paid, nor have we the means of paying them; if we had English gold, we might perhaps make our way to Paris."

"Our men are not so mercenary, Stofflet," said Bonchamps, "I do not think they have shewn any great desire for plunder."

"No," said Stofflet, "but they must live; if they are to have neither pay nor plunder, how are they to get to Paris?"

"I agree with you, Bonchamps," said Henri, "come what, come may, I would make a dash at Paris; we shall be cut to pieces here, while we are waiting for English aid; some of the men would follow us—most of them I believe; where we meet with friends, they will give us provisions; where we find enemies, we will take them, and pay the owners in republican assignats; they would get no other payment in the market-towns. I am sorry to disagree with you, Charles, but my voice is for Paris."

"And mine also, certainly," said Adolphe, "let our career be short, at any rate let it be glorious; let us march to Paris and strike terror into the tyrants of the Convention."

"It is difficult to strike terror into tyrants," said de Lescure quickly, "when the number of their supporters is ten times greater than that of their opponents."

"Well, Cathelineau," said Bonchamps, "what do you say? it is for you to settle the question between us; are we to go forward to Paris, or march back to Nantes?"

"I would wish to hear what others say; for myself, I fear that M. de Lescure is right. I fear the peasants would not follow us so far from their own homes. What does the Prince de Talmont say?"

"I will have no voice in the matter," said the Prince. "I have joined you but lately, and as yet am only fit to follow where others lead."

"And you, M. d'Elbée?" said Cathelineau.

"I hardly know how to speak," said d'Elbée, "where the subject is so important."

"M. d'Elbée is not wont to be so modest," said Stofflet; "does he not trust that Providence will inspire him with wisdom, when he opens his mouth to give his opinion?"

"Certainly, Stofflet; I trust in that all-seeing eye, at which you are so willing to scoff; but I do not expect that I am to be allowed to see further into futurity than another; however, if I am to express an opinion, I think we should endeavour to march on Paris; if we find that the men desert us, and that others do not join our standards, we must return."

"And how are we to return," said de Lescure, "and to whom? think you that we can collect another army in La Vendée, when one has deserted us on the road? will the peasants again trust in us, after they have once left us? Never If the army dissolves itself in despair, you will never be able to establish it again."

"Who talks of despair, Charles?" said Henri, "you did not despair when you were thundering against the gates of Saumur with four republicans to one royalist opposed to you; why should you despair now; or why should the army despair; I believe they would go anywhere at the command of their priests, and with the hope of restoring the King to his throne."

The question was then put to the vote. De Lescure and four others, voted for attacking Nantes. Bonchamps, and five others, declared for proceeding at once to Paris, with the view of arresting the present leaders of the Convention. Cathelineau was then called on to express his opinion, which would of course be decisive.

"I think M. de Lescure is right," said he, "I think we are not in a position to advance to Paris. I have not the heart to ask the men to follow me into a strange country, so far from their own homes."

The numbers were now equally divided, but as Cathelineau was the Commander-in-Chief, his voice turned the scale; and the expedition to Paris was postponed.

"So be it," said Bonchamps; "let us prepare then for Nantes; it is not fortified like Saumur, but the troops there are very numerous."

It was then decided that Cathelineau should name six lieutenants under him, to take command of the different districts from which the army was collected, and to which the men would be sure to return; and also appoint an officer in command of the artillery, and another in command of the cavalry. Cathelineau would have willingly dispensed with the task of selecting his officers—a work in which he could hardly fail to give offence to some, and in which he might probably give entire satisfaction to none; but it was to be done, and he felt that it was useless for him to shrink from it.

"M. Bonchamps," said he, "will of course take the command of the men of Anjou, and M. de Lescure of those from the southern parts of the Bocage, and they will assist me, I hope, in selecting the others. It is very difficult to select, where so many are fit."

"Rather say," said Henri, laughing, "where so many are equally unfit. Why, Bonchamps and Marigny are the only soldiers by profession we have among us."

"You'll all be soldiers shortly," said Father Jerome. "You are at any rate going the right way to learn the trade."

"Marigny of course will take the artillery," said Bonchamps. "We are very lucky in having so good an artillery officer among us."

"There is no one, at any rate, to dispute your claim, Marigny," said de Lescure.

"So he's president over 'Marie Jeanne' and the gunpowder," said Henri; "that's settled, isn't it Cathelineau?"

"Unless M. Marigny refuses," said Cathelineau.

"I am not modest enough for that, General," said Marigny. "Do you furnish me with guns, and I'll fight them. Do you collect the gunpowder, and I'll consume it."

"And the Prince de Talmont will take the cavalry?" said Cathelineau.

"No, indeed," said the Prince. "I will not interfere with Henri Larochejaquelin."

"Henri Larochejaquelin is much obliged to you, Prince," said Henri, "but he is not ambitious of making a fool of himself; nor does he wish to be made a fool of. Moreover, Henri Larochejaquelin does not wish to quarrel with an old friend like you, Prince; but he might be tempted to do so, if you take any liberties with his name."

"But, Cathelineau," said the Prince, "Henri has been at the head of the cavalry all through."

"Don't set a bad example, Prince," said de Lescure. "Let every man coincide with Cathelineau's directions without a word; so shall we be spared the ill effects of over modesty, and of too much assurance."

"Besides," said Cathelineau, "M. Larochejaquelin will be much wanted elsewhere. As a matter of course, he will be the leader of all the parishes round Chatillon; I doubt if the men would follow any one else."

"Dear Cathelineau," said Henri, "if you will take my advice, you will not make leaders of us youngsters at all. Adolphe and I will be well contented to be hussars for awhile. Let these grey-headed seniors be our leaders," and he pointed to d'Elbée whose hair was grizzled.

Henri had seen that the spirit of jealousy was already rising in Adolphe Denot's face. No allusion had been made to his services; his advice had never been asked in the council; there was no probability that he would be named as one of the leaders; he had hardly spoken a word since they had assembled in the council-room. Henri, though his own heart was a stranger to the jealousy and dread of neglect which tormented Adolphe, sympathised with, and felt for his friend; and he thought that if they were both together excluded from command at his request, the blow would be less keenly felt. They were the two youngest in the room, and their youth was a good reason why they should not be named; but Henri was the younger of the two, and he knew that if he were selected as one of the chiefs, Adolphe would be miserable at finding himself left out.

De Lescure, however, would not allow of this. He had promised that he would not disgrace Denot, by telling of the cowardice he had shewn at the Bridge of Fouchard, and he was determined to keep his word; but he would not allow his cousin, his pupil, his bosom friend, the man whom he loved with the affection of a brother and a father, to sink himself to the same level as a coward.

"How absurd is this!" said he, angrily. "I wonder, Henri, that you should be the first to create such foolish difficulties, when our very existence depends on perfect unanimity. In proportion as our means of enforcing obedience is slender, should our resolution be firm, implicitly to obey the directions of those who are selected as our leaders. We have made Cathelineau our General, and desired him to select his officers, and when he selects you as one, you object. If you object from a proper modesty, it argues that those who accept, shew an improper degree of assurance. You should think of these things, Henri."

"I resign myself to my dignity, and am dumb," said Henri laughing. "Go on, Cathelineau, and if the men you name, say but one word, one syllable against your choice—I'll slay them."

Cathelineau knew that all his difficulty still lay before him; those whom he had already chosen would as a matter of course be among the number; but who were to be the other three?

"M. Donnissan," said be, in a whisper to de Lescure, who was sitting next to him. "I do not know what his wishes might be."

"My father-in-law feels himself too old," answered de Lescure; "d'Elbée would be a much fitter person; he is thought so much of at Beauprieu."

"And the other two?" asked Cathelineau.

"Name one yourself, and ask Bonchamps to name the other."

"M. d'Elbée," said Cathelineau, aloud, "you will not, I am sure, refuse to take your portion of our labours."

"You will find," whispered Stofflet to his neighbour, "that as Providence has called upon him, he will be willing enough."

"I will do my best," said d'Elbée "as I am called upon; and may the Lord direct me, that I may fight His battle so as to do honour to His name."

"I think I will name Stofflet," said Cathelineau, consulting with Bonchamps and de Lescure; "he is a brave man, and though rude in his manner, he will make perhaps the best soldier among us; already the men obey him almost more implicitly than any one."

"Do—do!" said Bonchamps; "you cannot do better."

"I think you will be right to do so," said de Lescure, "though I do not like the man; but the peasants know him, and he is one of themselves. Yesterday morning I had ample proof of his courage. As you say, he is a brave man and a good soldier."

Stofflet was then informed that he had been named, and though he muttered some expressions as to his own want of the necessary qualifications, he was evidently well pleased that the choice had fallen on him.

And now the last of the lot was to be chosen. As the two last names had been mentioned, Denot's brow had grown blacker and blacker. Henri Larochejaquelin, during the whole proceeding, had been walking about the room, sitting now in one place, and now in another. At the present moment, he was sitting next to Adolphe, who, when Stofflet's name was mentioned, whispered to him, but almost audibly:

"Gracious heaven! Stofflet!—the whole affair is becoming discreditable. How can any gentleman serve under such a man as that?"

"You think too much of rank, Adolphe," said Henri; "we should entirely forget all distinctions of person now; unless we do so we can never succeed."

"But do you think we are more likely to set the King upon his throne, by making such a brute as that a General? I wonder whom our Commander-in-Chief will choose next—Foret, I suppose."

After having again consulted for some time, Bonchamps said to Cathelineau: "I do not think you can do better than name Adolphe Denot."

This was said in a low voice, but Adolphe's ears were not slow to catch his own name, and he was once more happy. Though he was named last, he would be equal with the others.

"Not so," said de Lescure, who had no idea that Denot had overheard the mention of his name, "Adolphe is not yet sufficiently known to the people; besides we have hitherto forgotten one, who though absent, we must not forget—one who was the first in the field against the Republic, who is already at the head of an army, and who has on various occasions shown himself capable to lead an army. We must not forget Charette."

The last words were spoken out loud, and though they were eagerly responded to by every one else, they fell with a heavy sound on Adolphe Denot's ear. To know that he was excluded after he had been named, to feel that he had been proposed merely to be rejected; it was more than he could bear; and as soon as Cathelineau had formally announced the name of M. Charette as one of their leaders, he started abruptly from his chair and said:

"Oh, of course, gentlemen, if you prefer Charette, so be it! He, doubtless will be better able to assist your endeavours than I should; but you might have spared me the mortification of putting my name on your list of officers, merely to scratch it off again."

"What matters it, Adolphe," said Larochejaquelin, blushing for his friend, "will you not share my command? Will not your word be as influential in the parishes of Chatillon as my own?"

"I sincerely beg your pardon, M. Denot," said Cathelineau, "if I have hurt your feelings, but you are as much aware as we are that we should be very wrong to neglect the merits of M. Charette; his achievements claim from us this distinction, and his power and influence would probably be lost to La Vendée, if we did not now incorporate his army with ours."

"I have nothing further to say," said Denot. "I must own I do not altogether admire the selection which has been made; but I have nothing further to say on the subject."

"I am sorry, Adolphe, that you have said so much," said de Lescure.

"You would have been apt to say more yourself if you had been passed over," said Adolphe, forgetting in his passion how he had disgraced himself before de Lescure at the bridge of Fouchard.

"I fear you misunderstand the purpose, which has collected here in Saumur so many men in arms," said he. "I fear that you think the peasants of our country have turned themselves into soldiers, that we might become generals, and play at being great men. Indeed, such is not the case; if personal ambition has brought you here, you had better leave us. We have come here to fight, and very probably to die for our King and our religion;

and, being called upon to act as leaders, we must bear a heavier share of the burden, and undergo greater perils than others; but we seek no especial dignity, we look for no other pre-eminence, than that of suffering more than others. I fear these are not the feelings that influence you."

"My feelings, Sir, are as pure as your own!" said Denot.

"If so," said Father Jerome, "you had better teach us all to think so, by taking care that your conduct is also as pure as M. de Lescure's."

"Oh, Father Jerome, do not anger him," said Henri. "Come with me, Adolphe, and we will quietly talk over this; they don't exactly understand what you mean yet."

"But they shall understand what I mean," said Denot, whose anger was now beyond control, "and they shall know that I will not remain here to be rebuked by a priest, who has thrust himself into affairs with which he has no concern; or to make myself subservient to men who are not fit to be my equals. I will not deign to be a common soldier, when such a man as Stofflet is made an officer."

And he got up from the chair in which he had again seated himself, and stalked out of the room.

"He has at any rate proved to us," said Bonchamps, "that I was wrong to nominate him, and that you were right not to accept the nomination."

"I grieve that he should be vexed with me," said Stofflet; "but I did not seek to put myself above him."

"Time and experience will make him wise," said de Lescure: "let us pity his folly and forgive it."

The council was then broken up, and the different officers went each to perform his own duties. When Denot left the room, Henri immediately followed him.

"Adolphe," said he, as he overtook him in the market-place, "Adolphe, indeed you are wrong, no one meant to show you any indignity."

"And have you also followed me to tell me I am wrong—of course I am wrong—I am wrong because I will not submit, as you and Charles do, to ignorant boors like Stofflet and Cathelineau, because—"

"Like Cathelineau! why, Adolphe, you are mad," said Henri, "why you yourself voted that Cathelineau should be our General."

"Voted! Why, Henri, what a child you are! Do you call that voting when all was arranged beforehand? You are blind, I tell you. You will vote next, I suppose, that your great General's valour shall de rewarded with your sister's hand!"

"My sister's hand! what is it you are speaking of?"

"Yes, Agatha's hand! think you that when you make a General of such as him, that his ambition will rest there? if you are content to be lieutenant to a postillion, I presume you will feel yourself honoured by a nearer connexion with him."

"Denot, you are raving mad! Cathelineau looking for my sister's hand?"

"Yes, Agatha's hand, the postillion looking for your sister's hand; and, Sir, you will find that I am not mad. Before long, Cathelineau will look for Agatha's hand: her heart he has already," and without waiting for any further answer, he hurried away.

"He must be raving mad," said Henri, "unlucky in love, and thwarted in ambition, he is unable to bear his griefs like a man. What a phantasy has jealousy created in his brain But Agatha was right; a man who could speak of her, even in his madness, as he has now spoken, was not worthy of her. Cathelineau! were he ten times lower than a postillion by birth, he would still be twenty times made noble by achievements and by character, and yet I would not wish—but nonsense! he thinks no more of wedding Agatha than I of Diana."

CHAPTER III
RETURN TO DURBELLIÈRE

When Adolphe Denot left his friend Henri in the street of Saumur, and ran off from him, Henri was so completely astonished by his parting words, so utterly dumb-founded by what he said respecting Agatha, that he made no attempt to follow him, but returned after awhile to the house, in which he, Charles and Adolphe were lodging, and as he walked slowly through the streets, he continued saying to himself, "Poor fellow, he is mad! he is certainly raving mad!"

From that time, no tidings whatsoever were heard of Denot. He had never returned to his lodging, nor been seen anywhere, except in the stable, in which his horse had been put to stand—he had himself saddled his horse, and taken him from the stall, and from that moment nothing further could be learnt of him in Saumur. De Lescure and Henri made the most minute inquiries—but in vain; had he destroyed himself, or hid himself in the town, his horse would certainly have been found; it was surmised that he had started for Paris on some mad speculation; and though his friends deeply grieved at his misconduct, his absence, when they had so much to do and to think of was in itself, felt as a relief.

After remaining about a week in Saumur, the army was disbanded—or rather disbanded itself, for every effort was made, to keep together as great a body of men as possible. An attempt was made to garrison the town; and for this purpose, the leaders undertook to pay about one thousand men, at a certain rate per day, for their services, while they remained under arms in Saumur, but the idea, after a very short time, was abandoned; the men would not stay away from their homes, and in spite of the comforts which were procured for them, and the pay which was promised, the garrison very quickly dissolved.

Cathelineau succeeded in taking back with him to St. Florent, nearly all the men who had accompanied him; his next object was the attack of Nantes, and as St. Florent is between Saumur and that town, his men were able to return to their homes, without going much out of their direct way. He marched through the town of Angers on his return, and took possession of the stores which he found there, the republican garrison having fled as soon as they heard of his approach; many of Bonchamps' men accompanied him, and some of those who had come to Saumur with de Lescure and Henri Larochejaquelin, young men who had no wives or families, and who literally preferred the excitement of the campaign, to their ordinary home employments; all such men joined Cathelineau's army, but by far the greater number of the peasants of the Bocage returned with de Lescure and Larochejaquelin.

Charette had been invited to assist Cathelineau in his attack on Nantes, and he had promised to do so; de Lescure found it absolutely necessary to go home, on account of his wound, and Larochejaquelin went with him. They had already heard that the Convention had determined to invade La Vendée on every side with an overwhelming force, and it was necessary to protect the Southern portion of the province; this duty was allotted to our two friends, and they therefore returned home from Saumur, without expecting to enjoy for any length of time the fruits of their recent victory.

A litter was formed for de Lescure, for at present he found it impossible to bear the motion of riding, and Henri, the little Chevalier, Father Jerome and Chapeau, accompanied him on horseback. Many of the peasants had started from Saumur, before their party, and the whole road from that town through Dou and Vihiers to Durbellière, was thronged with crowds of these successful warriors, returning to their families, anxious to tell to their wives and sweethearts the feats they had accomplished.

They were within a league of Durbellière, and had reached a point where a cross-road led from the one they were on to the village of Echanbroignes, and at this place many of the cortege, which was now pretty numerous, turned off towards their own homes.

"M. Henri," said Chapeau, riding up to his master, from among two or three peasants, who had been walking for some time by his horse's side, and anxiously talking to him, "M. Henri?"

"Well, Jacques; what is it now?" said Henri.

"I have a favour to ask of Monsieur."

"A favour, Chapeau; I suppose you want to go to Echanbroignes already, to tell Michael Stein's pretty daughter, of all the gallant things you did at Saumur."

"Not till I have waited on you and M. de Lescure to the château. Momont would be dying if he had not some one to give him a true account of what has been done, and I do not know that any one could give him a much better history of it, than myself—of course not meaning such as you and M.

de Lescure, who saw more of the fighting than any one else; but then you know, M. Henri, you will have too much to do, and too much to say to the Marquis, and to Mademoiselle, to be talking to an old man like Momont."

"Never fear, Chapeau. You shall have Momont's ears all to yourself; but what is it you do want?"

"Why, nothing myself exactly, M. Henri; but there are two men from Echanbroignes here, who wish you to allow them to go on to Durbellière, and stay a day or two there: they are two of our men, M. Henri; two of the red scarfs."

"Two of the red scarfs!" said Henri.

"Yes, M. Henri, two of the men who went through the water, and took the town; we call ourselves red scarfs, just to distinguish ourselves from the rest of the army: your honour is a red scarf that is the chief of the red scarfs; and we expect to be especially under your honour's protection."

"I am a red scarf, Henri;" said the little Chevalier. "There are just two hundred of us, and we mean to be the most dare-devil set in the whole army; won't we make the cowardly blues afraid of the Durbellière red scarfs!"

"And who are the two men, Jacques?" said Henri.

"Jean and Peter Stein," said Jacques: "you see, M. Henri, they ran away to the battle, just in direct opposition to old Michael's positive orders. You and the Curé must remember how I pledged my honour that they should be at Saumur, and so they were: but Michael Stein is an awful black man to deal with when his back is up: he thinks no more of giving a clout with his hammer, than another man does of a rap with his five knuckles."

"But his sons are brave fellows," said the little Chevalier, "and dashed into the water among the very first. Michael Stein can't but be proud that his two sons should be both red scarfs: if so, he must be a republican."

"He is no republican, Chevalier," said Chapeau, "that's quite certain, nor yet any of the family; but he is a very black man, and when once angered, not easy to be smoothed down again; and if M. Henri will allow Jean and Peter to come on to Durbellière, I can, perhaps, manage to go back with them on Sunday, and Michael Stein will mind me more than he will them: I can knock into his thick head better than they can do, the high honour which has befallen the lads, in their chancing to have been among the red scarfs."

"Well, Chapeau, let them come," said Henri. "No man that followed me gallantly into Saumur, shall be refused admittance when he wishes to follow me into Durbellière."

“We were cool enough, weren’t we, Henri, when we marched into the town?” said the Chevalier.

“We’ll have a more comfortable reception at the old château,” said Henri; “at any rate, we’ll have no more cold water. I must say, Arthur, I thought the water of that moat had a peculiarly nasty taste.”

They were not long in reaching the château, and Henri soon found himself in his sister’s arms. A confused account, first of the utter defeat of the Vendeans at Varin, and then of their complete victory at Saumur, had reached Durbellière; and though the former account had made them as miserable, as the latter had made them happy, neither one nor the other was entirely believed. De Lescure had sent an express to Clisson immediately after the taking of the town, and Madame de Lescure had sent from Clisson to Durbellière; but still it was delightful to have the good news corroborated by the conquerors themselves, and Agatha was supremely happy.

“My own dear, darling Henri,” she said, clinging round his neck, “my own brave, gallant brother, and were you not wounded at all—are you sure you are not wounded?”

“Not a touch, not a scratch, Agatha, as deep as you might give me with your bodkin.”

“Thank God! I thank Him with all my heart and soul: and I know you were the first everywhere. Charles wrote but a word or too to Victorine, but he said you were the very first to set your foot in Saumur.”

“A mere accident, Agatha; while Charles had all the fighting—the real hard, up hill, hand to ‘hand work—I and a few others walked into Saumur, or rather we swam in, and took possession of the town. The Chevalier here was beside me, and was over the breach as soon as I was.”

“My brave young Arthur!” said Agatha, in her enthusiasm, kissing the forehead of the blushing Chevalier, “you have won your spurs like a knight and a hero; you shall be my knight and my hero. And I will give you my glove to wear in your cap. But, tell me Arthur, why have you and Henri, those red handkerchiefs tied round your waist? Chapeau has one too, and those other men, below there.”

“That’s our uniform,” said Arthur. “We are all red scarfs; all the men who clambered into Saumur through the water, are to wear red scarfs till the war is over; and they are to be seen in the front, at every battle, seige and skirmish. Mind, Agatha, when you see a red scarf, that he is one of Henri Larochejaquelin’s own body-guard; and when you see a bald pate, it belongs to a skulking republican.”

"Are the republicans all bald then?" said Agatha.

"We shaved all we caught at Saumur, at any rate. We did not leave a hair upon one of them," said Arthur, rejoicing. "The red scarfs are fine barbers, when a republican wants shaving."

"Is Charles badly wounded?" asked Agatha.

"His arm is broken, and he remained in action for eight hours after receiving the wound, so that it was difficult to set; but now it is doing well," said Henri.

"I should have offered him my services before this: at any rate I will do so now; but Henri I have a thousand things to say to you; do not expect to go to bed tonight, till you have told me everything just as it happened," and Agatha hurried away, to give her sweet woman's aid to her wounded cousin, while Henri went into his father's room.

"Welcome, my hero! welcome, my gallant boy!" said the old man, almost rising from his chair, cripple as he was, in his anxiety to seize the hand of his beloved son.

"I have come home, safe, father," said Henri, "to lay my sword at your feet."

"You must not leave it there long, Henri, I fear, you must not leave it there long; these traitors are going to devour us alive; to surround us with their troops and burn us out of house and home; they will annihilate the people they say, destroy the towns, and root out the very trees and hedges. We shall see, Henri—we shall see. So they made a bad fight of it at Saumur?"

"They had two men to one against us, besides the advantage of position, discipline and arms, and yet they marched the best part of their troops off in the night without striking a blow."

"Thanks be to the Lord, we will have our King again; we will have our dear King once more, thanks be to the Almighty," said the old man, eager with joy. "And they fled, did they, without striking a blow!"

"Some of them did, father; but some fought well enough; it was desperate sharp work when poor Charles was wounded."

"God bless him! God bless him! I didn't doubt it was sharp work; but even with valour, or without valour, what could sedition and perjury avail against truth and loyalty! they were two to one; they had stone walls and deep rivers to protect them; they had arms and powder, and steel cuirasses; they had disciplined troops and all the appanages of war, and yet they were scattered like chaff; driven from their high walls and deep moats, by a few half-armed peasants; and why? why have our batons been more deadly than their swords? because we have had truth and loyalty on our side. Why have our stuff jackets prevailed against their steel armour; because they covered honest hearts that were fighting honestly for their King. His Majesty shall enjoy his own again, my boy. Vive le Roi! Vive le Roi!"

"I trust he may, father; but, as you say, we shall have some hard work to do first. Cathelineau and Charette will be before Nantes in a week's time. I should have been with them had we not heard that a strong body of republican troops is to be stationed at Parthenay. They say that Santerre is to command a party of Marseillaise, commissioned to exterminate the Vendeans."

"What, Santerre, the brewer of the Faubourgs?"

"The same, Danton's friend, he who used to be so loud at the Cordeliers; and Westerman is to assist him," said Henri.

"Worse again, Henri, worse again; was it not he who headed the rebels on the tenth of August, when our sainted King was driven from his home?"

"Yes, the same Westerman is now to drive us from our homes; or rather to burn us, our homes, and all together—such at least is the task allotted to him."

"God help our babes and our women!" said the old Marquis shuddering, "if they fall into the clutches of Santerre, and that other still blacker demon!"

"Do not fear, father; have we not shewn that we are men? Santerre will find that he has better soldiers to meet than any he brings with him."

"Fear, Henri! no, for myself I fear nothing. What injury can they do to an old man like me? I do not even fear for my own children; if their lives are required in the King's service, they know how to part with them in perfect confidence of eternal happiness hereafter; but, Henri, I do feel for our poor people; they are now full of joy and enthusiasm, for they are warm from victory, and the grief of the few, who are weeping for their relatives, is lost in the joy of the multitude. But this cannot always be so, we cannot expect continual victory, and even victory itself, when so often repeated, will bring death and desolation into every parish and into every family."

"I trust, father, the war will not be prolonged so distantly as you seem to think; the forces of Austria, England and Prussia already surround the frontiers of France; and we have every reason to hope that friendly troops from Britain will soon land on our own coast. I trust the autumn will find La Vendée crowned with glory, but once more at peace."

"God send it, my son!" said the Marquis.

"I do not doubt the glory—but I do doubt the peace."

"We cannot go back now, father," said Henri.

"Nor would I have you do so; we have a duty to do, and though it be painful we must do it. 'God will temper the wind to the shorn lamb,' and give us strength to bear our sufferings; but my heart shudders, when I am told that the Republic has let loose those wolves of Paris to shed the blood of our poor people."

The prospect of a prolonged civil war, of continued strife, and increased bloodshed, somewhat damped the joy with which the victory at Saumur was discussed in the aristocratic portion of the château; but no such gloomy notions were allowed to interfere with the triumph which reigned in the kitchen. Here victory was clothed in robes all couleur de rose, and it appeared that La Vendée, so happy in many other respects, was chiefly blessed in being surrounded by republicans whom she could conquer, and in having enemies who gave her the means of acquiring glory.

"And our own young master was the first royalist who put his foot in Saumur?" asked Momont, who had already received the information he required four or five times, and on each occasion had drunk Henri's health in about half-a-pint of wine.

"Indeed he was," said Chapeau, "the very first. You don't think he'd have let any one go before him."

"Here's his health then, and God bless him!" said Momont. "It was I first showed him how to fire a pistol; and very keen he was at taking to gunpowder."

"Indeed, and indeed he was," said the housekeeper. "When he was no more than twelve years old, not nigh as big as the little Chevalier, he let off the big blunderbuss in my bed-room, and I on my knees at prayers the while. God bless his sweet face, I always knew he'd make a great soldier."

"And don't you remember," said the laundress, "how he blew up Mademoiselle Agatha, making her sit on a milk-pan turned over, with a whole heap of gunpowder stuffed underneath, and she only six or seven years old?"

"Did he though," said the page, "blow up Mademoiselle Agatha?"

"Indeed he did, and blew every scrap of hair off her head and eyebrows. It's no wonder he's such a great general."

"And the Chevalier was second, wasn't he?" said the cook.

"Dear little darling fellow!" said the confidential maid; "and to think of him going to the wars with guns and swords and pistols! If anything had happened to him I should have cried my eyes out."

"And was the Chevalier the first to follow M. Henri into the town?" asked the page, who was a year older than Arthur Mondyon, and consequently felt himself somewhat disgraced at not having been at Saumur.

"Why," said Jacques, with a look which was intended to shew how unwilling he was to speak of himself, "I can't exactly say the Chevalier was the first to follow M. Henri, but if he wasn't the second, he was certainly the third who entered Saumur."

"Who then was the second?" said one or two at the same time.

"Why, I shouldn't have said anything about it, only you ask me so very particularly," said Jacques, "but I believe I was second myself; but Jean Stein can tell you everything; you weren't backward yourself Jean, there were not more than three or four of them before you and Peter."

"I don't know about that," said Jean, "but we all did the best we could, I believe."

"And was Chapeau really second?" said Momont, who was becoming jealous of the distinction likely to be paid to his junior fellow-servant. "You don't mean to say he went in before all the other gentlemen?"

"Gentlemen, indeed!" said Chapeau. "What an idea you have of taking a town by storm, if you think men are to stand back to make room for gentlemen, as though a party were going into dinner."

"But tell us now, Jean Stein," continued Momont, "was Chapeau really second?"

"Well then," said Jean, "he was certainly second into the water, but he was so long under it, I doubt whether he was second out—he certainly did get a regular good ducking did Chapeau. Why, you came out feet uppermost, Chapeau."

"Feet uppermost!" shouted Momont, "and is that your idea of storming a town, to go into it feet uppermost?"

"But do you really mean to say that you were absolutely wet through when you took Saumur?" said the laundress.

"Indeed we were," answered Chapeau, "wringing wet, every man of us."

"Lawks! how uncomfortable," said the cook. "And M. Henri, was he wet too?"

"Wet, to be sure he was wet as water could make him."

"And the little Chevalier, did he get himself wet?" said the confidential maid, "poor little fellow! it was like to give him his death of cold."

"But, Chapeau, tell me truly now: did you kill any of those bloody republicans with your own hand?" asked the housekeeper.

"Kill them," said Chapeau, "to be sure, I killed them when we were fighting."

"And how many, Chapeau; how many did you positively kill dead, you know?" said the confidential maid.

"What nonsense you do talk!" answered he, with a great air of military knowledge, "as if a man in battle knows when he kills and when he doesn't. You're not able to look about you in that sort of way in the middle of the smoke and noise and confusion."

"You don't mean to tell me you ever kill a man without knowing it!" said the housekeeper.

"You don't understand what a battle is at all," answered Chapeau, determined to communicate a little of his experience on the matter. "One hasn't time to look about one to see anything. Now supposing you had been with us at the taking of Saumur."

"Oh, the Lord forbid!" said the housekeeper. "I'd sooner be in my grave any day, than go to one of those horrid bloody battles."

"Or you, Momont; supposing you'd been there?"

"Maybe I might have done as much as another, old as I look," replied the butler.

"I'm sure you'd have done well, Momont. I'm sure you'd have done very well," endeavouring to conciliate him into listening; "but supposing you had been there, or at the camp of Varin—we'll say Varin, for after all, we had more fighting there than at Saumur. Supposing you were one of the attacking party; you find yourself close wedged in between your two comrades right opposite the trenches; you have a loaded musket in your hand, with a bayonet fixed to it, and you have five or six rounds of cartridges in your belt; you know that you are to do your best, or rather your worst with what you've got. Well, your commander gives the word of attack. We'll suppose it's the good Cathelineau. 'Friends,' he will say; 'dear friends; now is the time to prove ourselves men; now is the moment to prove that we love our King; we will soon shew the republicans that a few sods of turf are no obstacles in the way of Vendean royalists,' and then the gallant fellow rushes into the trenches; two thousand brave men follow him, shouting 'Vive le Roi!' and you, Momont, are one of the first. All of a sudden, as you are just in motion, prepared for your first spring, a sharp cutting gush of air passes close to your face, and nearly blinds you; you feel that you can hardly breathe, but you hear a groan, and a stumble; your next neighbour and three men behind him have been sent into eternity by a cannon-ball from the enemy. Do you think then that the man who fired the cannon knows, or cares who he has killed? Well, on you go; had you not been in a crowd, the enemy's fire, maybe, might have frightened you; but good company makes men brave: on you go, and throw yourself into the trench. You find a more active man than yourself just above you; he is already nearly at the top of the bank, his feet are stuck in the sods above your head; he is about to spring upon the rampart, when the bayonet of a republican passes through his breast, and he falls at your feet, or perhaps upon your head. You feel your heart shudder, and your blood runs cold, but it is no time for pausing now; you could not return if you would, neither can you remain where you are: up you go, grasping your musket in one hand and digging the other into the loose sods. Your eyes and mouth are crammed with dust, your face is bespattered with your comrade's blood, your ears are full of strange noises; your very nature changes within you; the smell of gunpowder and of carnage makes you feel like a beast of prey. You do not think any longer of the friends who have fallen beside you; you only long to grapple with the enemy who are before you."

"Oh, mercy me! how very shocking!" said the housekeeper. "Pray don't go on Chapeau; pray don't, or I shall have such horrid dreams."

"Oh! but you must go on, Chapeau," said the confidential maid, "I could never bear that you should leave off; it is very horrid, surely; but as Mademoiselle says, we must learn to look at blood and wounds now, and hear of them, too."

"Do pray tell us the rest," said the page, who sat listening intently with his mouth wide open. "I do so like it; pray tell us what Momont did after he became a beast of prey?"

Chapeau was supremely happy; he felt that his military experience and his descriptive talents were duly appreciated, and he continued:

"Well, you are now in the camp, on the enemy's ground, and you have to fight every inch, till you drive them out of it; six or seven of your comrades are close to you, and you all press on, still grasping your muskets and pushing your bayonets before you: the enemy make a rush to drive you back again; on they come against you, by twenties and by thirties; those who are behind, push forward those who are in front, and suddenly you find a heavy dragging weight upon your hands, and again you hear the moans of a dying man close to you—almost in your arms. A republican soldier has fallen on your bayonet. The struggles of the wounded man nearly overpower you; you twist and turn and wrench, and drag your musket to and fro, but it is no use; the weapon is jammed between his ribs; you have not space nor time to extricate it; you are obliged to leave it, and on you go unarmed, stumbling over the body of your fallen enemy. Whether the man dies or lives, whether his wound be mortal or no, you will never hear. And so you advance, till gradually you begin to feel, rather than to see, that the blues are retreating from you. You hear unarmed men asking for quarter, begging for their lives, and the sound of entreaty again softens your heart; you think of sparing life, instead of taking it; you embrace your friends as you meet them here and there; you laugh and sing as you feel that you have done your best and have conquered; and when you once more become sufficiently calm to be aware what you are yourself doing, you find that you have a sword in your hand, or a huge pistol; you know not from whom you took them, or where you got them, or in what manner you have used them. How can a man say then, whom he has killed in battle, or whether he has killed any man? I do not recollect that I ever fired a shot at Varin myself, and yet my musket was discharged and the pan was up. I will not say that I ever killed a man; but I will say that I never struck a man who asked for mercy, or fired a shot even on a republican, who had thrown down his arms."

Henri's voice was now heard in the hall, loudly calling for Jacques, and away he ran to join his master, as he finished his history.

"It makes my blood run cold," said the housekeeper, "to think of such horrid things."

"Chapeau describes it very well, though," said the confidential maid; "I'm sure he has seen it all himself. I'm sure he's a brave fellow."

"It's not always those who talk the most that are the bravest," said Momont.

Henri and his sister sat talking that night for a long time, after the other inhabitants of the château were in bed, and though they had so many subjects of interest to discuss, their conversation was chiefly respecting Adolphe Denot.

"I cannot guess what has become of him," said Henri; "I made every possible inquiry, short of that which might seem to compromise his character. I do not think he can have returned to the Bocage, or we should have heard of him."

"He must have gone to Fleury," said Agatha. "I am sure you will not find that he is at his own house."

"Impossible, my love; we must have heard of him on the way; had he gone round by Montrenil, he must still have passed over the bridge of Fouchard, and we should have heard of him there."

"He must have ridden over in the night; you see he so evidently wanted to conceal from you where he was going."

"My own impression is, that he is gone to Paris," said Henri; "but let him have gone where he may, of one thing I am sure; he was not in his right senses when he left the council-room, nor yet when he was speaking to me in the street; poor Adolphe! I pity him with all my heart. I can feel how miserable he must be."

"Why should he be miserable, Henri? The truth is, you mistake his character. I do not wish to make you think ill of your friend; but Adolphe is one of those men whom adversity will improve. You and our father have rather spoilt him between you; he is too proud, too apt to think that everything should bend to his wishes: he has yet to learn that in this world he must endure to have his dearest wishes thwarted; and till adversity has taught him that, his feelings will not be manly, nor his conduct sensible."

"Poor fellow!" said Henri, "if adversity will teach him, he is likely to get his lesson now. Did he part quietly with you, Agatha, on the day before we started to Saumur?"

"Anything but quietly," said she. "I would not tell you all he said, for on the eve of a battle in which you were to fight side by side, I did not wish to make you angry with your friend and companion: but had a raging madman, just escaped from his keepers, come to offer me his hand, his conduct could not have been worse than Adolphe Denot's."

"Was he violent with you, Agatha?"

"He did not offer to strike me, nor yet to touch me, if you mean that: but he threatened me; and that in such awful sounding, and yet ridiculous language, that you would hardly know whether to laugh or to be angry if I could repeat it."

"What did he say, Agatha?"

"Say! it would be impossible for me to tell you; he swung his arms like a country actor in a village barn, and declared that if he were not killed at Saumur, he would carry me away in spite of all that my friends could do to hinder him."

"Poor fellow! poor Adolphe!" said Henri.

"You are not sorry I refused him? You would, indeed, have had to say, poor Agatha! had I done otherwise."

"I am not sorry that you refused him, but I am sorry you could not love him."

"Why you say yourself he is mad: would you wish me to love a madman?"

"It is love that has made him mad. Adolphe is not like other men; his passions are stronger; his feelings more acute; his regrets more poignant."

"He should control his passions as other men must do," said Agatha: "all men who do not, are madmen." She remained silent for a few moments, and then added, "you are right in saying that love has made him mad; but it is the meanest of all love that has done so—it is self-love."

"I think you are too hard upon him, Agatha; but it is over now, and cannot be helped."

"What did he say to you, Henri, when he left you in Saurnur?"

"His name had been mentioned you know in the council as one of the leaders: Bonchamps, I believe, proposed it; but Charles objected, and named Charette in his place, and Cathelineau and the rest agreed to it. This angered Adolphe, and no wonder, for he is ambitious, and impatient of neglect. I wish they would have let him been named instead of me, but they would not, and when the list was finished, he was not on it. He got up and said something; I hardly know what, but he complained of Stofflet being one of the Generals; and then Charles rebuked him, and Adolphe in a passion left the room."

"And you followed him?" asked Agatha.

"Yes, I followed him; but he was like a raging madman. I don't know how it was; but instead of complaining about the Generals, he began complaining about you. I don't know exactly whether I ought to tell you what he said—indeed I had not intended to have done so."

"Nay, Henri; now you have raised my woman's curiosity, and you positively must tell me."

"I hardly know how to tell you," said Henri, "for I really forget how he said it. I don't know on earth how he introduced your name at all; but he ended in accusing you of having a more favoured lover."

Agatha blushed slightly as she answered:

"He has no right whatever to ask the question; nor if I have a favoured lover, should it be any ground of complaint to him. But to you, Henri, if you wish a promise from me on the subject, I will readily and willingly promise, that I will receive no man's love, and, far as I can master my own heart, I will myself entertain no passion without your sanction: and you, dear brother, you shall make me a return for my confidence; you shall ask me to marry no man whom I cannot love."

"Don't for a moment think, dearest, that what he said, made me uneasy as regarded you: but whom do you think he selected for you—of whom do you think he is jealous?"

"I cannot attempt to guess a madman's thoughts, Henri."

"I will tell you then," said he; "but you will be shocked as well as surprised. He is jealous of Cathelineau!"

"Cathelineau?" said Agatha, blushing now much more deeply than she had done before.

"Yes, Cathelineau, the postillion."

"No, not Cathelineau the postillion; but Cathelineau the Saint of Anjou, and the hero of St. Florent, and of Saumur. He at any rate has linked my name with that of a man worthy of a woman's love."

"Worthy, Agatha, had his birth and early years been different from what they were."

"Worthy as he is of any woman's love," said Agatha. "Great deeds and noble conduct make birth of no avail, to give either honour or disgrace."

"But, Agatha, surely you would not wed Cathelineau, were he to ask you?"

"Why should you ask that question, Henri?" said she: "are the words which Adolphe Denot has uttered in his wild insanity of such weight, as to make you regard as possible such an event? Have I not told you I would wed no one without your sanction? Do you not know that Cathelineau has never spoken to me but the coldest words of most distant respect? Do you not know that his heart and soul are intent on other things than woman's love? I, too, feel that this is not the time for love. While I live in continual dread that those I most value may fall in battle; while I fear that every messenger who comes to me in your absence, may have some fatal news to tell, I do not wish to take upon me a fresh burden of affection. Am I not best as I am, Henri, at present?" And she put her arm affectionately through his. "When the wars are over, and the King is on his throne, you shall bring me home a lover; some brave friend of your's who has proved himself a gallant knight."

"I would have him be a gallant knight, certainly," said Henri, "but he should also be a worthy gentleman."

"And is not Cathelineau a worthy gentleman?" forgetting in her enthusiasm that she was taking the cause of one who was being spoken of as her lover. "Oh, indeed he is; if valour, honesty, and honour, if trust in God, and forgetfulness of self, if humanity and generosity constitute a gentleman, then is Cathelineau the prince of gentlemen: but do not, pray do not mistake me, Henri: a lover of scenery admires the tops of distant mountains, and gazes on their snowy peaks with a pleasure almost amounting to awe; but no one seeks to build his house on the summit: so do I admire the virtues, the devotion, the courage of Cathelineau; but my admiration is mixed with no love which would make me wish to join my lot with his. I only say, that despite his birth and former low condition, he is worthy of any woman's love."

Henri did not quite like his sister's enthusiasm, though he hardly knew why it displeased him. He had thought of Cathelineau only as a soldier and a General, and had found nothing in him that he did not approve of; but he felt that he could not welcome him as his darling sister's husband; "if Adolphe should have prophesied rightly," said he, to himself as he went from his sister's room to his own chamber, "but no! whatever her feelings may be, she is too good to do anything that would displease me."

CHAPTER IV
MICHAEL STEIN

On the Sunday morning, after Henri's return to Durbellière, Jacques Chapeau, with Jean and Peter Stein, left the château very early, and started for Echanbroignes. Word had been sent to the old smith by some of the neighbours, who had been at Saumur, that his two sons were safe and sound, and that they had behaved well at the siege, and a message at the same time reached Annot, informing her that Jacques meant to spend his next Sunday at the village; the party was therefore expected, and great preparations were made for a fête at Echanbroignes. The heroes of that place considered that they had somewhat celebrated themselves; in the first place, on final inquiry, it appeared, that not one person from the village, who was at all able to go to Saumur, had neglected to do so. In the next place, many of the villagers were among the number of the red scarfs, and they claimed to themselves the privilege of being considered peculiarly valiant and particularly loyal; and lastly, though many of them had gone to Saumur, without arms, every man on his return had a musket with him, which the old men and women regarded as absolute trophies, taken by each man individually from some awful rebel whom he had slain in single combat. There were to be great rejoicings, therefore, at Echanbroignes, which were postponed for the arrival of Chapeau and the two Stems.

The old smith was very angry at his sons' behaviour. As Chapeau had said, he was a very black man, and when he was angered, it wasn't easy to smooth him; the operation, however, was attempted by some of his neighbours, and though they were not altogether successful, they succeeded in making the old man a little proud of his family.

"Yes, Paul Rouel;" he said to the village innkeeper, who was an ancient crony of his, "it's very well to talk of King and Church; but if King and Church are to teach sons to fly against their fathers, we may, I think, have a little too much of them; didn't I again and again tell the boys not to go?"

"But, Michael Stein, how could you expect them to stay here, with a score of old men like us, and a number of women and girls, when every young fellow in the parish had gone to the wars? besides, they say, they did gallantly at the wars, and gained great honour and glory."

"Gained a great fiddle-stick," said the smith.

"But, Michael Stein," said another old friend, named Gobelin, "you wouldn't have your children disgraced, would you? think how sheepish they would have looked, hiding themselves in the smithy here, when all the other young men were parading round the green with the guns and swords they have taken from the rebels, and the women and girls all admiring them. Why, neighbour, not a girl in the parish would have spoken to them."

"Girls spoken to them, indeed! I tell you, Gobelin, in the times now coming, any girl will be ready enough to speak to a young man that has a house over his head, and a five-franc piece in his pocket. No, neighbour Gobelin; I gave my boys a good trade, and desired them to stick to it; they have chosen instead to go for soldiers, and for soldiers they may go. They don't come into my smithy again, that's all."

"You don't mean you won't speak to the lads, and after their fighting so bravely and all!" said Paul Rouel, in a voice of horror.

"I didn't say I wouldn't speak to them, Rouel," said the father, "I am as fond of my sons as another man; and as they were resolved to disobey my commands, and to go fighting, why I'll not say but I'm glad they didn't disgrace themselves. I'd have been sorry to hear that they'd run away, or been the last to face the enemy; but they had no right to go, when there was work for them to do at home; they are welcome now to come and take the best I can give them, till their new trade calls them away again, and then they'll be welcome to go soldiering again; not a hammer shall they raise on my anvil, not a blast shall they blow in my smithy, not an ounce of iron shall they turn in my furnace."

"You'll think better of these things after a day or two, neighbour," said Gobelin.

"When I think once about a thing, Gobelin, I'm not much given to think again. But I tell you, I wish the boys no harm; let them be soldiers now, and I pray God they may be good soldiers; only, if I save a little money by hard work, I won't have them spend it among their comrades in strong drink; it'll be all the better for Annot, when I die, that's all."

In this resolution he remained fixed, and in this frame of mind he received his truant sons on their return to Echanbroignes on the Sunday morning. They entered the village together with Chapeau, about nine in the morning, having been met about a mile from the town, by four or five friends, who escorted them back. Annot was not there, for she was very busy at home, preparing breakfast for her brothers and lover. She at any rate was determined that the prodigal sons should be received with a fatted calf.

Chapeau marched up through the village at the head of the little procession to bear the brunt of the father's anger, as his station in life, and standing in the army made him feel superior even to the fury of old Michael Stein. As they approached the door of the smith's house, they saw him sitting in the little porch with a pipe in his mouth, for Michael was never found without one or two implements; he had always either his hammer or his pipe in lull activity.

"Welcome back to Echanbroignes, M. Chapeau, welcome back," said the old man. "I am heartily glad to see so brave a soldier in my poor cabin!" and he gave his hand to Jacques.

"And here be two other brave soldiers, Michael Stein, who, I hope, are also welcome to Echanbroignes; and this I will say, any father in Poitou might be proud to own them for his Sons: for gallanter fellows there are not in the whole army of La Vendée, and that is saying a long word."

There was a little crowd round the smith's house, and in spite of his unmilitary predilections, he could not help feeling proud at the public testimony that was paid to his sons' merits: he showed this by the tear that stood in his eye, as he said:

"They are welcome too, M. Chapeau; they are very welcome too. I am glad to see ye, safe and sound from the wars, lads. I am glad to see thee, Jean: I am glad to see thee, Peter," and he gave a hand to each of the two young men, who were delighted with their unexpected kind reception. "And this I will say before the neighbours here, as ye would go to the wars, and make soldiers of yourselves, I am well pleased to hear ye behaved yourselves like gallant brave men should do. I'd sooner that your friends should have had to tell me that ye were both stiff and cold, than that ye should have returned yourselves with shamed faces to own that ye had disgraced the trade ye have chosen to take up with."

"Bravo! Bravo!" said Chapeau, "I am glad in my heart, Michael Stein, to hear you speak so kindly to the lads; and so will M. Henri be glad to hear it, for they are two of his own especial troop—they are two of the gallant red scarfs, who swam into Saumur with their muskets tucked under their arms."

"But understand me, boys," continued the smith, still speaking so that the neighbours standing round could hear him. "I am right glad to see both of you, as I am to see M. Chapeau, or any other gallant friend who is kind enough to visit me and Annot. But mind, it is as visitors I receive you; in a few days, doubtless, you must go away to the wars again; till then ye shall have the best I can give, both to eat and to drink. Ye shall have your own way, and never be asked to do a turn of work. Ye shall have gay holyday times, and holyday fare, and anything the old man can do, and anything the old man can give to make you merry, he will do, and he will give, because you have come back gallantly, and have not brought dishonour to the roost where ye were hatched—but more than this I will not agree to. Ye would not abide at home, as I desired, and this therefore is no longer a home for you; ye would not be content to be forgers of weapons, but ye must e'en use them too, and ye have had your way. Now, lads, I must have my way; and for the rest of the time I must have it alone. This is no longer your home, lads, and I am no longer your master. Ye would be soldiers when I did not wish it; now let ye be soldiers, and I'm the less sorry for it, as it seems like that you'll prove good soldiers. And now, Peter and Jean, you're welcome both of you. Jacques Chapeau you are most heartily welcome—come Annot, let the lads have a swinging breakfast, for I know these soldiers fight not well unless they be fed well," and so finishing his speech, he led the way into the cottage.

The three men were too well pleased with their reception to grumble at the smith's mode of expressing his feeling. Jean and Peter were delighted to find that they were to be entertained with the best their father could afford, instead of with black looks and hard words, and that the only punishment to be immediately inflicted on them, was that they were to do no work; the party, therefore, entered the cottage tolerably well pleased with each other.

It is not to be supposed that Annot remained in the back-ground during the whole of her father's oration. She had come out of the cottage, and kissed her two brothers, and shaken hands with her lover; she then returned in again, and Chapeau had followed her, and as the two were left alone together, for a minute or two, I think it very probable that she kissed him also; but I cannot speak positively on this point.

Then they all sat down to breakfast, and Paul Rouel and old Gobelin, who had contrived to be of the party, were greatly surprised to hear and to see how civil Michael was to his sons. He pressed them to eat of the very best, as he did to Chapeau, and talked to them about the war, listened to all their tales, and had altogether lost the domineering authoritative tone of voice, with which he usually addressed his own family; it was only in talking to Annot that he was the same hot-tempered old man as ever. The two young men themselves were hardly at their ease; but they eat their breakfast, and made the best they could of it.

"Smothered fire burns longest, neighbour Gobelin," said Rouel, as he left the house. "Take my word, Michael will never forgive those two boys of his the longest day he has to live."

After breakfast, Michael Stein and his whole party went to mass, as did all the soldier peasants, who had returned from Saumur; and the old Curé of the parish, who had now recovered possession of his own church, with much solemnity returned thanks to God for the great victory which the Vendeans had gained, and sung a requiem for the souls of the royalists who had fallen in the battle. When they left the church, the peasants all formed themselves into a procession, the girls going first, and the men following them; and in this manner they paraded round the green, carrying a huge white flag, which had been embroidered in the village, and which bore in its centre, in conspicuous letters of gold, those three words, the loyal Shibboleth of La Vendée, "Vive le Roi!"

This flag they fixed on a pole erected in the centre of the green, and then they set to work to amuse themselves with twenty different games. The games, however, did not flourish—the men were too eager to talk of what they had done, and the girls were too willing to listen—they divided themselves into fifty little parties, in which fifty different accounts were given of the taking of Saumur, and in each party three or four different warriors were named as having been the most conspicuous heroes of the siege. Each narrator had some especially esteemed leader or chief, who in his eyes greatly exceeded the other leaders, and the prodigious feats of valour performed by this favoured warrior was the first and most wonderful subject of discourse. Then, but at a modest distance, as regards the glory of the achievements related, each peasant told what he had done himself; two or three probably made out their little history together, and told of each other's valour: that homely and somewhat vulgar Scotch proverb, "you scratch my back, and I'll scratch yours," was certainly unknown to them, but nevertheless they fully recognized the wise principle of mutual accommodation which that proverb teaches.

"It's no use talking, but there isn't one of them able to hold a candle to our M. Henri—is there, Louis? that is, for a downright thundering attack."

This was said by Jean Stein to two or three of the village girls, by whom he was looked on as a great hero, in consequence of his having gone to the war in spite of his father's commands, as well as on account of Chapeau's honourable testimony in his favour; and the man referred to, was one Louis Bourdin, who, as well as Jean, had been of the party who followed Henri through the moat.

"That there is not, Jean; that is, for positive standup fighting; not one. And we ought to know, for we have seen most of 'em. There's Cathelineau is a very good man at leading on the men."

"Oh, yes!" said Jean, "Cathelineau is a fine fellow too, and a very holy man; but somehow I don't think he's quite so forward as M. Henri. M. Henri is always the first."

"But doesn't he get dreadfully knocked about by the guns and bullets?" asked one of the girls.

"He doesn't matter that a pinch of snuff," said Louis.

"No, not a pinch of snuff," said Jean. "Do you mind, Louis, how he leapt off his horse, and dashed through the trenches, that first night at Varin? wasn't it beautiful?"

"You may say that, Jean," answered Louis; "it was beautiful. And what a night that was—you were along with him, Jean, and so was Chapeau. M. Henri was up first, I can swear to that; but it would puzzle any one to say who was second."

"Yourself Louis, was as quick as any one—I marked you well. Indeed then, said I to myself, if all our men are as forward as Louis Bourdin, the village will have a great name before the war is over."

"But tell me truly now, Louis Bourdin," said a little girl, who was listening intently all the time, "when you went up into that place, were there real soldiers in armour, with guns and cannon firing at you all the time?"

"Truly then there were, Lolotte, hundreds of them," said Bourdin.

"Well, that is horrible!" said the girls all at once.

"And do you remember, Jean," continued Bourdin, "when M. Henri dashed down again, how the traitor rebels hallooed out, 'Fire upon the red scarf!' Well, I did think it was all up with him then. You were close to him, Jean; nearer than I am to Lolotte now."

"And that's quite near enough," said Lolotte, giving him a push.

"Why I'm sure I was doing nothing; I was only wanting to show you. Jean Stein there, was, as I was saying, quite close to M. Henri; and as they leapt out of the camp together, twenty voices roared out at once, 'Fire upon the red scarf! fire upon the red scarf!' Oh! that was a fearful evening; it was dark then, and the light of the smoking, glaring torches made it five times more horrible. I thought we were as good as dead men then. I'm sure I for one can't guess how we ever got out alive."

"And yet, M. Henri wasn't wounded," said Jean; "well it was wonderful. After all, General d'Elbée must be right; Providence must give a shake to a rebel's arm, just as he's firing, so as to send his bullet anywhere but where it's meant to go."

"Yes," said Bourdin, "and it directs the shot of a royalist right into a rebel's heart."

"Well, if that be so," said Lolotte, "I'm sure I for one wouldn't like to fight on the rebel's side. They must be wonderful brave men to hold out at all, when Providence goes against them in that way."

"But they don't hold out, girl," said Jean, "they always run away; how they did run, Bourdin, when M. Henri led us into the town, through the broken wall; well, I believe they all thought at that time, the devil himself was coming for them out of the moat."

"Only think, girls, three or four thousand men running away as fast as their feet could carry them, from two hundred fellows, who hadn't a charge of dry powder among them, and who were all themselves dripping wet through; well that was fine."

Jacques Chapeau and Annot Stein had not joined any of these parties; they had disappeared soon after mass, and were not heard of for three or four hours afterwards; they took a long ramble by themselves, down by the mill-stream, and far beyond the mill; sitting down, every now and then among the willows, and then getting up and strolling on a bit further; they did not, this day, waste their time in foolish quarrels and fond reconciliations; but discoursed together, sundry serious matters of important business, as becomes people to do, when they think of arranging a partnership concern, from which each intends to get a comfortable means of living for the remainder of his or her life; upon the whole, they had but very few subjects of difference, and by their return to the smith's house at supper-time, they had fully agreed that no further time ought to be lost, in establishing a firm under the name of Jacques and Annot Chapeau and Co. The Co. being left to come afterwards or not, as God might please.

After supper was over, Annot had no difficulty in inducing her brothers to leave the house, and thus the coast was left clear for Jacques to ask the father's consent to his intended marriage. Neither he nor Annot expected much difficulty in persuading Michael to accept of so promising a son-in-law; but they were both determined that if they could not marry with his consent, they would do so without it. So Chapeau lighted his pipe, and sat himself down opposite the smith, and Annot retired to her own little sleeping chamber, where she might conveniently hear what her father and lover said to each other, respecting her intended nuptials.

"Well, Michael Stein, my old friend," said Jacques; "these are glorious times, are they not? The rebels beaten hollow, till they haven't a face to shew for themselves, and the King coming to La Vendée, to enjoy his own again; it will be a fine thing to see the King riding into the village of Echanbroignes to thank the gallant peasants, with his own mouth, for what they have done for him!"

"Yes, M. Chapeau! those will be fine times when they come; pray God you, and other young fellows like you, may live to see them; an old fellow like me has little chance of such happiness."

"And why not, my friend? what is to make those days so far off? I tell you, Michael Stein, the rebels were dead beaten at Saumur; they are scattered like chaff; their very best soldiers are altogether hors de combat; the war is as good as over. We may have to make a little trip or two, just to receive the English, who are coming to help us; we may have to go and meet them on the coast; or perhaps to Parthenay, to ask M. Santerre what he wants in that part of the world; but that is all, literally all; I tell you the rebels are clean beaten."

"I only wonder then, M. Chapeau, why you want the English to come and help you, if, as you say, you have conquered all the republicans yourselves?"

"Just to pay their respects to the King, and, perhaps, to lend us a hand in driving those Jacobins out of Paris—that's all. Till that's done the King is to live at Saumur."

"To live at Saumur, is he?"

"That's what those say who know most about it, and you know I'm in the way to know what's really going forward. He's to hold his court at Saumur, and Henri Larochejaquelin is to be commandant of the town, and have the command of all the forces there. I tell you, Michael Stein, we, that wear the red scarfs, will not be the worse off then."

"I hope not; in truth, M. Chapeau, I hope not; though they do say that they be not wise who put their trust in princes."

"Princes!" said Jacques, "I am not talking of princes, I am talking of the King himself, God bless him!"

"Well, perhaps, that does make a difference; and I say, God bless him too, with all my heart."

"I suppose you've heard, Michael Stein, that our young General, M. Henri, is going to be married?"

"Is he then?" said Michael. "No, truly, I did not hear a word of such a matter; to some grand lady of the court, I suppose?"

"No, but to his own beautiful young cousin, Mademoiselle de Lescure, the sister of our other General, you know."

"Well, may they be happy, both of them; I mind their fathers well; the old Marquis is still alive, but greatly ailing they tell me. I have much to be thankful for, and I do thank the Lord!" and as he spoke, Michael Stein crossed himself. "Now, I'm as old in a manner as the Marquis himself and yet you see I can still make the big hammer clink on the anvil."

"Indeed you can, Michael, and better too than many a young fellow. But, as we were saying, here is M. Henri going to be married, and his lady will surely be wanting some nice, tidy, handy, good-looking, smart young woman to be about her, more as a sort of a companion, you know, than a servant; in the same way, you mind, as I am now to M. Henri: now, wouldn't that be a nice berth for your daughter, Annot Stein?"

As Chapeau described the nice, tidy, smart, pretty young woman, that the future Madame de Larochejaquelin would be sure to require, Annot smoothed down her little apron with both her hands, gave a complaisant glance at her own neat little feet, and her bright holiday shoes, and then listened eagerly for her father's answer.

"I am sure, M. Chapeau, that Annot Stein is very thankful for your good wishes," said he, "and so is her father, very thankful; but she has not court-breeding enough for that sort of work; she has never learnt to speak smooth, and say pretty little flattering sayings, such as ladies like to hear. Nor when Madame would be out of sorts and ruffled, as great ladies will be sometimes, would she know how to say the right word just at the right time; and then Annot has too much of her father's rough blood, and if Madame scolded at all, it's ten chances to one, but she would scold again, and that, you know, wouldn't do. No, M. Chapeau, Annot had better remain as she is, and keep her father's house, till she marries some honest tradesman, like myself, when these deadly wars be over."

"Well, but my dear friend," said Chapeau, "I had another little proposition I wanted to make, which would fit in so well with what I suggested; and I can assure you Madame Henri, that is Mademoiselle de Lescure as she is now, you know, is the softest, sweetest-tempered creature living—she wouldn't quarrel with any one, much less with such a little angel as your daughter."

"I'm sure," said Michael, making a low bow to his guest, and pressing the handle of his pipe to his breast. "I'm sure my daughter will be very thankful for the great interest you take respecting her."

"But as I was saying, you know, about this other little proposition of mine?"

"Well, M. Chapeau, I'm listening with all my ears, and very thankful for your kind friendship."

"You see," said Jacques, "M. Henri is going to change his condition; we've both been young fellows together; we've had our amusements and our pleasures like other young men, and, maybe, been as fortunate as most. Well, my friend, M. Henri is going to settle down, and marry the girl of his heart, whom he loves better than all the world; and what can I do better than follow his example? The truth is, I mean to settle down too, Michael Stein."

"Well," said Michael, scratching his head, and listening for the remainder of Chapeau's little proposition.

"And I want to marry the girl of my heart, whom I love better than all the world, and her name is Annot Stein, and there's an end of it; and now you know all about it."

Annot's heart beat quickly as she heard him make the last important declaration; and beautifully she thought he made it. When Chapeau called her a little angel, she swore to herself that he was the dearest fellow that ever lived and when he finished by protesting that she was the girl of his heart, and that he loved her better than all the world, she longed to run out and throw her arms about his neck.

Michael Stein took a long pull at his pipe, and blew out a huge cloud of tobacco before he made any answer, and then he said:

"M. Chapeau, I am sensible how great an honour you propose to do me and my poor daughter; but I am not a proud man, no one can say that Michael Stein was ever proud or ambitious; my only wish is to see my little girl married to a decent hard-working fellow, like her father."

"Well, ain't I a hard-working fellow?"

"Let me look at your hands, M. Chapeau; the inside of your hands. No, you are not a hard-working fellow; your hand is as soft as a lady's."

"What signifies my hand? I shan't make a worse husband, shall I, because my hand is not as horny as your own."

"No, but a hard-fisted fellow is the only man that will suit my daughter."

"But, Michael Stein, she herself thinks—"

"Who ever heard of asking a girl what she thinks herself? Of course she'd sooner be a fine lady, and spend her time walking about a big chateau than be milking cows and minding goats."

"But won't she be earning her living and her wages honestly?"

"Wages! I don't like those sort of wages, M. Chapeau. I don't mean to say anything uncivil, and I hope you won't take it amiss, but there are two trades I don't fancy for my children: the one is that of a soldier, the other that of a great man's servant."

"Gracious me, Michael Stein! why I'm both," said Chapeau, rather offended.

"I beg your pardon again and again, and I really mean no offence: clown as I am, I hope I know better than to say anything to hurt my own guest in my own house."

Chapeau assured him he was not offended, and begged to know why the old man objected to see his children become soldiers or servants.

"They've no liberty," said Michael, "though they usually take a deal too much licence. They never are allowed to call their time their own, though they often misuse the time that ought to belong to other people."

For a long time Chapeau combatted such arguments as these, but without avail; the smith declared that now, as his two sons had become soldiers, it would break his heart if his daughter also were to marry one. He assured Jacques, with tears running down his rough cheeks, that he could not bring himself to give his daughter his blessing, if she left his house without his leave to marry a soldier. He declared that he also loved her better than all the world, and that he could not bear to part with her; and his tears and kindly words had such an effect upon Annot, that she could not restrain herself: she burst into tears herself and running out of her little room, threw herself into her father's arms.

"Get up, thou simpleton; get up, thou little fool," said he. "Why, Annot, what ails thee?"

"Oh, father! dear father!" said she.

"Get up then, Annot, and I'll speak to thee. I never saw thee in this way before."

"Oh, father!" she said, sobbing violently, "do you love your poor daughter so very, very much?"

"Love you, Annot! why yes, I do love you. If you'll be a good girl, that is, I will love you."

"I will be a good girl, dear father; indeed I'll be a good girl; at any rate I'll try. But then—" and she stood up, and commenced wiping her eyes with her little apron.

"Well, what then, Annot?" said the smith.

"But then—I wouldn't anger you, father, for all the world; indeed I wouldn't, for you always are so good to me, and I know I don't deserve it," and poor Annot continued sobbing and rubbing her eyes with her apron.

"Nonsense, girl, nonsense!" said Michael; "I don't find any fault with you. Don't think of getting yourself married till these wars be over, that's all," and he kissed her forehead, and patted her cheek as though all the difficulty were over.

"But, father—?" continued Annot, with her apron still to her face.

"Well, child, what is it? By the blessed mass, M. Chapeau, I don't know what the girl's crying for."

"Do you love your own little Annot so very, very much?" said she, and she put her soft arm round his rough neck, and placed her cheek quite close to his.

"There, Annot; why what nonsense, girl! Don't you know I love you? didn't you hear me say so this minute? Leave off, will you, you little slut! why, what will M. Chapeau think of us? Well, I declare she's crying still!"

"But if you really, really love me, father—"

"Bother the girl! she knows I love her better than anything else; God forgive me."

"If you really love me," repeated Annot, nestling her head in her father's bosom, "you must, you must, you must—do something that I'll ask you, father."

"And what is it, child? I doubt much it's nonsense."

"You must love Jacques Chapeau too, father," and having uttered these important words, Annot clung fast to her father's arms, as if she feared he was going to throw her off, and sobbed and cried as though her heart were breaking.

The battle between the contending factions, namely, the father on one side, and the daughter with her lover on the other, was prolonged for a considerable time, but the success was altogether with Annot. Chapeau would have had no chance himself against the hard, dry, common sense of the smith; but Annot made her appearance just at the right moment, before the father had irrevocably pledged himself, and the old man was obliged to succumb; he couldn't bring himself to refuse his daughter when she was lying on his bosom and appealing to his love; so at last he gave way entirely, and promised that he would love Jacques Chapeau also; and then Chapeau, he also cried; and, I shudder as I write it, he also kissed the tough, bronzed, old wiry smith, and promised that he would be a good husband and son-in-law.

As soon as Annot had got her wish, and had heard Jacques received as her betrothed husband, she also was wonderfully dutiful and affectionate.

She declared that she didn't want to be married till the wars were nearly over, and the country was a little more quiet; that she would never go away and leave her father altogether, and that if ever she did go and live at Durbellière, she would certainly make an agreement with her master and mistress that she should be allowed to walk over to eat her dinner with her father every Sunday.

As soon as the smith found himself completely conquered, he resigned himself to his fate, and became exceedingly happy and good-humoured. He shook Chapeau's hand fifty times, till he had nearly squeezed it off. He sent to the inn for two bottles of the very best wine that was to be had; he made Annot prepare a second supper, and that not of simple bread and cheese, but of poached eggs and fried bacon, and then he did all that he possibly could to make Chapeau tipsy, and in the attempt he got very drunk himself, and so the day ended happily for them all.

CHAPTER V
THE HOSPITAL OF ST. LAURENT

De Lescure only remained three days at Durbellière, and then started again for his own house at Clisson, and Henri accompanied him. They had both been occupied during these three days in making such accommodation as was in their power for the sick and wounded, who were brought back into the Bocage in considerable numbers from Saumur. The safe and sound and whole of limb travelled faster than those who had lost arms and legs in the trenches at Varin, or who had received cuts and slashes and broken ribs at the bridge of Fouchard, and therefore the good news was first received in the Bocage; but those miserable accompaniments of victory, low tumbrils, laden with groaning sufferers lying on straw, slowly moving carts, every motion of which opened anew the wounds of their wretched occupants, and every species of vehicle as could be collected through the country, crammed with the wounded and the dying, and some even with the dead, were not long in following the triumphal return of the victorious peasants.

A kind of hospital was immediately opened at a little town called St. Laurent sur Sèvre, about two leagues from Durbellière, at which a convent of sisters of mercy had long been established. De Lescure and Larochejaquelin between them supplied the means, and the sisters of the establishment cheerfully gave their time, their skill, and tenderest attention to assuage the miseries of their suffering countrymen. Agatha knew the superior of the convent well, and assisted in all the necessary preparations. She was there when the hospital was first opened, and for a long time afterwards visited it once or twice a week, on which occasions she stayed for the night in the convent; had it not been that she could not bring herself to leave her father, she would have remained there altogether, as long as the war continued to supply the little wards with suffering patients. They were seldom, or rather never, empty as long as the Vendeans kept their position in the country, the sick and the wounded were nursed with the tenderest care at St. Laurent. The sisters who had commenced the task never remitted their zeal, nor did Agatha Larochejaquelin. The wards were by degrees increased in number, the building was enlarged, surgical skill was procured, every necessary for a hospital was obtained, whatever might be the cost, and whatever the risk; till at last, in spite of the difficulties which had to be encountered, the dangers which surrounded them, the slenderness of their means, and the always increasing number of their patients, the hospital of St. Laurent might have rivalled the cleanliness, care, and comfort of the Hotel Dieu in its present perfection.

As soon as the first arrangements for the commencement of this hospital had been made, de Lescure and Henri went to Clisson. It may easily be supposed that de Lescure was anxious to see his wife, and that she was more than anxious to see him. Henri also was not sorry to hear the praises of his valour sung by the sweet lips of Marie. He stayed one short happy week at Clisson, basking in the smiles of beauty, and they were the last hours of tranquillity that any of the party were destined to enjoy for many a long sad day. De Lescure's recovery was neither slow nor painful, and before the week was over, he was able to sit out on the lawn before the château, with one arm in a sling, and the other round his wife's waist, watching the setting of the sun, and listening to the thrushes and nightingales. Every now and again he would talk of the future battles to be fought, and of the enemies to be conquered, and of the dangers to be encountered; but he did not speak so sadly of the prospects of his party as he did when he had only just determined to take up arms with the Vendeans. The taking of Thouars, and Fontenay, of Montreuil, and Saumur, had inspirited even him, and almost taught him to believe that La Vendée would be ultimately successful in re-establishing the throne.

De Lescure was delighted to see what he thought was a growing attachment between his sister and his friend. Had he had the power of choosing a husband for Marie out of all France, he would have chosen Henri Larochejaquelin: he loved him already as he could only love a brother, and he knew that he had all those qualities which would most tend to make a woman happy.

"Oh, if these wars were but over," said he to his wife, "how I would rejoice to give her to him, he is such a brave and gallant fellow—but as tender-hearted and kind as he is brave!"

"These weary, weary wars!" said Madame de Lescure, with a sigh, "would they were over: would, with all my heart, they had never been begun. How well does the devil do his work on earth, when he is able to drive the purest, the most high-minded, the best of God's creatures to war and bloodshed as the only means of securing to themselves the liberty of worshipping their Saviour and honouring their King!"

Henri himself, however, had not considered the propriety of waiting until the wars were over before he took a wife for himself, or at any rate before he asked the consent of the lady's friends: for the day before he left Clisson, he determined to speak to Charles on the subject; though he had long known Marie so well, and had now been staying a week in the house, he had never yet told her that he loved her. It was the custom of the age and the country for a lover first to consult the friends of the young lady, and though the peculiar circumstances of his position might have emboldened Henri to dispense with such a practice, he was the last man in the world to take advantage of his situation.

"Charles," said he, the evening before his departure, as he stood close to the garden seat, on which his cousin was sitting, and amused himself with pitching stones into the river, which ran beneath the lawn at Clisson. "Charles, I shall be off tomorrow; I almost envy you the broken arm which keeps you here."

"It won't keep me long now, Henri," said he; "I shall be at Chatillon in a week's time, unless you and d'Elbée have moved to Parthenay before that. Cathelineau will by that time be master of Nantes, that is, if he is ever to be master of it."

"Don't doubt it, Charles. I do not the least: think of all Charette's army. I would wager my sword to a case-dagger, that Nantes is in his hands this minute."

"We cannot always have the luck we had at Saumur, Henri?"

"No," said Henri, "nor can we always have a de Lescure to knock down for us the gates of the republicans."

"Nor yet a Larochejaquelin to force his way through the breach," said the other.

"Now we are even," said Henri, laughing; "but really, without joking, I feel confident that the white flag is floating at this moment on the castle at Nantes; but it is not of that, Charles, that I wish to speak now. You have always been an elder brother to me. We have always been like brothers, have we not?"

"Thank God, we have, Henri! and I do not think it likely that we shall ever be more distant to each other."

"No, that I'm sure we never shall. You are too good either to quarrel yourself, or to let me quarrel with you; but though we never can be more distant, we may yet be more near to each other. You know what I mean, Charles?"

"I believe I do," said de Lescure; "but why do you not speak out? You are not likely, I think, to say or to propose anything that we shall not approve of—that is, Victorine and I."

"God bless you both!" said Henri. "You are too kind to me; but can you consent to give me your own dear favourite sister—your sweet Marie? You know what I mean in saying that I would be nearer to you."

De Lescure was in the act of answering his cousin, when the quick fall of a horse's foot was heard in the avenue close to the house, and then there was a sudden pause as the brute was pulled up violently in the yard of the château, and the eager voices of domestics answering the rapid questions of the man who had alighted.

Interested as the two friends were in their conversation, the times were too full of important matters to allow of their remaining quiet, after having heard such tokens of a hurried messenger. Larochejaqnelin ran off to the yard of the château, and de Lescure followed him as quickly as his wounded arm would allow.

Henri had hardly got off the lawn, when he met a couple of servants coming from the yard, and between them a man booted, spurred, and armed, covered with dust and spattered with foam, whom he at once recognized as Foret, the friend and townsman of Cathelineau.

"What news, Foret, what news?" said Henri, rushing up to him, and seizing him by the hand. "Pray God you bring with you good tidings."

"The worst news that ever weighed heavy on a poor man's tongue, M. Henri," said Foret, sorrowfully.

"Cathelineau is not dead?" said Henri, but the tone of his inquiry shewed plainly how much he feared what the reply would be.

"He was not dead," answered Foret, "when I left him five leagues on this side Nantes, but he had not many days to live."

The two had turned back over the lawn, and now met de Lescure, as he hastened to join them.

"Cathelineau," said Henri, "is mortally wounded! Victory will have been bought too dear at such a price; but I know not yet even whether the Vendeans have been victorious."

"They have not—they have not," said Foret. "How could they be victorious when their great General had fallen?"

"Mortally wounded! Oh, Foret, you are indeed a messenger of evil," said de Lescure, giving him his hand.

"Yes, mortally wounded," said Foret. "I fear before this he may have ceased to breathe. I left him, gentlemen, a few leagues this side Nantes, and at his own request hurried on to tell you these sad tidings. Oh, M. de

Lescure, our cause has had a heavy blow at Nantes, and yet at one time we had almost beaten them; but when the peasants saw Cathelineau fall, they would fight no longer."

"Where is he?" said Henri, "that is if he still lives."

"I crossed the river with him," answered Foret, "and brought him on as far as Remouille. He wished to be carried to the hospital you have opened at St. Laurent, and unless he has died since I left him, he is there now. I hurried on by Montacué and Tiffauges to St. Laurent; and there, M. Henri, I saw Mademoiselle Agatha, and told her what had happened. If there be an angel upon earth she is one! When I told her that the good Cathelineau was dying, every shade of colour left her beautiful cheek; she became as pale as marble, and crossed her hands upon her bosom; she spoke to me not a word, nor did I look for reply, for I knew that in her heart she was praying that his soul might be taken up to heaven."

Henri at that moment remembered the enthusiastic declaration of his sister, that Cathelineau, despite his birth, was worthy of any woman's love, and he did not begrudge her the only means which now remained to her of proving her devotion to the character she had admired.

"I told her," continued Foret, "that if he lived so long, Cathelineau would reach the hospital on the following day, and then I hurried on to you. She told me I should find you here. It was then dark, but I reached Chatillon that night, for they sent a guide with me from St. Laurent. I left Chatillon again at the break of day, and have not lost much time in arriving here."

"No, indeed, Foret; and surely you must need rest and refreshment," said de Lescure. "Come into the château, and you shall have both."

"But tell us, Foret, of this reverse at Nantes," said Henri. "I will at once start for St. Laurent; I will, if possible, see Cathelineau before he dies; but let me know before I go to him how it has come to pass that victory has at last escaped him."

"Victory did not escape him," said Foret: "he was victorious to the last—victorious till he fell. You know, gentlemen, it had been arranged that Nantes should be attacked at the same moment by Charette from the southern banks of the Loire, and by Cathelineau from the northern, but this we were not able to accomplish. Charette was at his post, and entered the town gallantly over the Pont Rousseau, but we were unable to be there at the appointed time. For ten hours we were detained by a detachment of the blues at the little town of Nort, and though we carried it at last, without losing many of our men, the loss of the precious hours was very grievous. We pushed on to Nantes, however, without losing another minute, and though we found the rebels ready to receive us, they could not hold their ground against us at all. We drove them from the town in every direction. We were already in the chief square of Nantes, assured of our victory, and leading our men to one last attack, when a musket ball struck Cathelineau on the arm, and passing through the flesh entered his breast. He was on foot, in front of the brave peasants whom he was leading, and they all saw him fall. Oh, M. de Lescure, if you had heard the groan, the long wail of grief, which his poor followers from St. Florent uttered, when they saw their sainted leader fall before them, your ears would never forget the sound. We raised him up between us, and carried him back to a part of the town which was in our hands, and from thence over the Pont Rousseau to Pirmil, where I left him for a while, and returned to the town, but I could not get the peasants to follow me again—that is, his peasants; and he was too weak to speak to them himself. It was not till two hours after that he was able to speak a word."

"And you lost all the advantage you had gained?" asked de Lescure.

"We might still have been successful, for the blues would always rather run than fight when they have the choice, but the Prince de Talmont, in his eagerness, headed the fugitive rebels who were making for Savenay, and drove them back into the town; when there, they had no choice but to fight; indeed, their numbers were so much greater than our own, that they surrounded us. Our hearts were nearly broken, and our arms were weak; it ended in our retreating to Pirmil, and leaving the town in the hands of the republicans."

"How truly spoke that General who said, 'build a bridge of gold for a flying enemy!'" said de Lescure.

"And is Cathelineau's wound so surely mortal?" asked Henri.

"The surgeon who examined him in Pirmil said so; indeed, Cathelineau never doubted it himself. He told me, as soon as he could speak, that he should never live to see the Republic at an end. 'But,' added he, 'you, Foret, and others will; and it delights me to think that I have given my life to so good a cause.'"

Henri's horse was now ready, and he made no longer delay than to say adieu to his hostess, and to speak one or two last words to his cousin Marie, and then he made the best of his way to Chatillon and St. Laurent, hoping once more to see Cathelineau before he died. All his spurring and his hurrying was in vain.

A few hours before Henri could reach the hospital, the Saint of Anjou had breathed his last, and Agatha Larochejaquelin had soothed his dying moments.

As Foret had related, Agatha, on hearing of Cathelineau's wound, had turned deadly pale. It was not love that made her feel that the world was darkened by his fall; that from henceforward nothing to her could be bright and cheerful; at least not such love as that which usually warms a woman's heart, for Agatha had never hoped, or even wished to be more to Cathelineau than an admiring friend; nor yet was it grief for the loss of services which she knew were invaluable to the cause she had so warmly espoused. These two feelings were blended together in her breast. She had taught herself to look to Cathelineau as the future saviour of her country; she loved his virtue, his patriotism, and his valour; and her heart was capable of no other love while that existed in it so strongly. The idea of looking on Cathelineau as a lover, of seeing him kneeling at her feet, or listening to him while he whispered sweet praises of her beauty, had never occurred to her; had she dreamed it possible that he could do so, half her admiration of him would have vanished. No, there was nothing earthly, nothing mundane in Agatha's love, for though she did love the fallen hero of La Vendée, the patriot postillion of St. Florent, she did not shed a tear when she heard that he was dragging his wounded body to St. Laurent, that he might have the comfort of her tender care in his last moments; her hand did not shake as she wrote a line to her father to say that she could not leave the hospital that evening, or probably the next; nor did she for one half hour neglect the duties which her less distinguished patients required her to perform; but still she felt her heart was cold within her, and that if God had so willed it, she could, without regret, take her place in the grave beside the stricken idol of her admiration, who had fallen at Nantes while fighting for his God and his King.

Early on the morning after Foret's departure for Clisson, the litter which bore the wounded chief reached the hospital, and Agatha's arm assisted him from the door-step to the death-bed, which she had prepared for him. Agatha's feelings towards him have been imperfectly described; but what were his feelings towards her? What was the nature of the mysterious love, which no kind words had ever encouraged, which no look had ever declared, which he had hardly dared to acknowledge to his own heart, and which had yet induced the wounded man to make so painful a journey, to travel over twenty long, long leagues, that he might once more see the glorious face which had filled his breast with such an unutterable passion? Not for a moment had he ever dreamt that Agatha regarded him differently than she did the many others who had taken up arms in the service of their country. His name he knew must be familiar to her ears, for chance had made it prominent in the struggle; but beyond that, it had never occurred to his humble mind that Agatha Larochejaquelin had given one thought to the postillion of St. Florent. For some time, Cathelineau had been unable to define to himself the passion which he felt, but had gradually become aware that he loved Agatha passionately, incurably, and hopelessly. Her image had been present to him continually; it had been with him in the dead of night, and in the heat of day; in the hour of battle, and at the council-table; in the agony of defeat, and in the triumph of victory. When he found himself falling in the square at Nantes, and all visible objects seemed to swim before his eyes, still he saw Agatha's beautiful pale face, and then she seemed to smile kindly on him, and to bid him hope. As soon as his senses returned to him, he was made conscious that he was dying, and then he felt that he should die more happily if he could see once more the fair angel, who had illuminated and yet troubled the last few days of his existence.

Cathelineau had heard that Agatha had taken under her own kind care the hospital at St. Laurent, but he had not expected that she would be on the step to meet him as he was lifted out of his litter; but hers was the first face he saw on learning that his painful journey was at an end. His wound had been pronounced to be inevitably mortal, and he had been told that he might possibly live for two or three days, but that in all probability his sufferings would not be protracted so long. The fatal bullet had passed through his arm into his breast, had perforated his lungs, and there, within the vitals of his body, the deadly missile was still hidden. At some moments, his agony was extreme, but at others, he was nearly free from pain; and as his life grew nearer to its close, his intervals of ease became longer, and the periods of his suffering were shortened. He had confessed, and received absolution and the sacrament of his church at Remouille; and when he reached St. Laurent, nothing was left for him but to die.

He tried to thank her, as Agatha assisted him to the little chamber which she had prepared for him; but his own feelings, and his exertions in moving were at first too much for him. The power of speech, however, soon returned to him, and he said:

"How can I thank you, Mademoiselle, what am I to say to thank you for such care as this?"

"You are not to thank us at all," said Agatha, (there was one of the sisters of mercy with her in the room). "We are only doing what little women can do for the cause, for which you have done so much."

Again he essayed to speak, but the sister stopped him with a kind yet authoritative motion of her hand, and bade him rest tranquil a while, and so he did. Sometimes Agatha sat by the window, and watched his bed, and at others, she stole quietly out of the room to see her other patients, and then she would return again, and take her place by the window; and as long as she remained in the room, so that he could look upon her face, Cathelineau felt that he was happy.

He had been at St. Laurent some few hours, and was aware that his precious moments were fast ebbing. He hardly knew what it was that he longed to say, but yet he felt that he could not die in peace without expressing to the fair creature who sat beside him the gratitude he felt for her tender care. Poor Cathelineau! he did not dream how difficult he would find it to limit gratitude to its proper terms, when the heart from which he spoke felt so much more than gratitude!

"Ah, Mademoiselle!" he began, but she interrupted him.

"Hush, hush, Cathelineau!" she said. "Did you not hear sister Anna say that you should not speak."

"What avails it now for me to be silent?" said he. "I know, Mademoiselle, that I am dying, and, believe me, I do not fear to die. Your kind care can make my last few hours tranquil and easy, but it cannot much prolong them. Let me have the pleasure of telling you that I appreciate your kindness, and that I give you in return all that a dying man can give—my prayers."

"And I will pray for you, Cathelineau," said Agatha. "But will not every Vendean pray for the hero who first led them to victory, who first raised his hand against the Republic?"

"How precious are the praises of such as you!" said he. "Pray for me and for your other poor countrymen who have fallen in this contest; such prayers as yours will assuredly find entrance into heaven."

He then again laid tranquil for a while, but his spirit was not quiet within him; he felt that there was that which he longed to say before he died, and that the only moments in which the power of speaking would be left to him were fast passing from him.

"Do not bid me be silent," he said; "did I not know that no earthly power could prolong my life, I would do nothing to defeat the object of my kind nurses; but as it is, a few moments' speech are of value to me, but an extra hour or so of torpid life can avail me nothing. Ah, Mademoiselle, though I cannot but rejoice to see our cause assisted by the nobility and excellence of the country, though I know that the angelic aid of such as thou art—"

"Stop, stop," said Agatha, interrupting him, "if you will speak, at any rate do not flatter; your last words are too precious to be wasted in such idleness."

"It does not seem to be flattery in me to praise you, Mademoiselle; heaven knows that I do not wish to flatter; but my rude tongue knows not how to express what my heart feels. I would say, that valuable as is your aid to our poor peasants, I almost regret to see you embarked in a cause which will bathe the country in blood, and which, unless speedily victorious, will bring death and desolation on the noble spirits who have given to it all their energies and all their courage."

"Do you think so badly, Cathelineau, of the hopes of the royalists?"

"If we could make one great and glorious effort," said he, and his eyes shone as brightly as ever while he spoke; "if we could concentrate all our forces, and fill them with the zeal which, at different times, they all have shewn, we might still place the King upon his throne, and the white flag might still wave for ages from our churches, as a monument of the courage of La Vendée. But if, as I fear, the war become one of detached efforts, despite the wisdom of de Lescure, the skill of Bonchamps, the piety of d'Elbée, the gallant enthusiasm of Larochejaquelin, and the devoted courage of them all, the Republic by degrees will devour their armies, will consume their strength, will desolate the country, and put to the sword even their wives and children: neither high nobility, nor illustrious worth, nor surpassing beauty will shield the inhabitants of this devoted country from the brutality of the conquerors, who have abjured religion, and proclaimed that blood alone can satisfy their appetites."

"Surely God will not allow his enemies to prevail," said Agatha.

"God's ways are inscrutable," answered Cathelineau, "and his paths are not plain to mortal eyes; but it is not the less our duty to struggle on to do those things which appear to us to be acceptable to Him. But should these sad days come, should atheism and the love of blood stride without control through our villages; if it be doomed that our houses are to be burnt and our women to be slaughtered, why should all remain to be a prey to our enemies? Ah, Mademoiselle leave this devoted country for a while, take your sweet cousin with you; bid M. de Lescure send away his young wife: it is enough that men should have to fight with demons; men can fight and die, and suffer comparatively but little, but female beauty and female worth will be made to suffer ten thousand deaths from the ruthless atrocities of republican foes."

Agatha shuddered at the picture which Cathelineau's words conjured up, but her undaunted courage was not shaken.

"God will temper the wind to the shorn lamb," said she. "Neither I, nor Marie will leave our brothers, nor will Madame de Lescure leave her husband; it is little we can do to hasten victory, but we can lessen suffering and administer comfort, when comfort is most required. Had you, Cathelineau, loved some woman above all others, and been loved by her;

had you had with you in your struggle some dear sister, or perhaps still dearer wife, would you have asked her to go from you, that you might have battled on, and struggled, and at last have died alone?"

"By God's dear love, I would," said he, raising himself, as he spoke, upon his bed. "My most earnest prayer to her should have been to leave me."

"And when she refused to do so; when she also swore by God's dear love, that she would stay with you till the last; as she would have done, Cathelineau, if she loved you as—as you should have been loved; would you then have refused the comfort her love so longed to give you?"

"I know not then what I would have done," said he, after lying with his eyes closed for a few moments without answering. "I have never known such love. Our women love their husbands and their brothers, but it is only angels love with such a love as that."

"Such is the love a man deserves who gives his all for his King and his country. If our husbands, and our brothers, and our dear friends, Cathelineau, are brave and noble, we will endeavour to imitate them; as long as there is an abiding-place for them in the country, there are duties for us. If God vouchsafed to spare you your life a while, that you might live to be the instrument of restoring His worship, do you think that I would run from your bedside, because I heard that the rebels were near you? Oh, Cathelineau! you do not know the passive courage of a woman's heart."

Cathelineau listened to her with all his ears, and gazed on her with all his eyes, as she spoke to him. It seemed to him as though another world had opened to his view even before his death; as though paradise could give him no holier bliss than to gaze on that face, and to listen to that voice.

"I never knew what a woman was till now," said he; "and how much better is it that I should die this moment, with your image before me, than return to a world, such as mine has been, where all henceforward would be distasteful to me."

"Should you live, Cathelineau, you would live to be honoured and valued. If it be God's pleasure that you should die, your memory will be honoured—and loved," said Agatha.

He did not answer her for a while, but lay still, with his eyes fixed upon her, as she sat with her elbow leaning on the window. Oh! what an unspeakable joy it was to him to hear such heavenly words spoken by her, whom he had almost worshipped; and yet her presence and her words turned his thoughts back from heaven to the earth which he had all but left. Could she really have loved him had it been his lot to survive these wars?

Could she really have descended from her high pinnacle of state and fortune to bless so lowly a creature as him with her beauty and her excellence? As these thoughts passed through his brain, he began for the first time to long for life, to think that the promised blessings of heaven hardly compensated for those which he was forced to leave on earth; but his mind was under too strong control to be allowed to wander long upon such reflections. He soon recovered his wayward thoughts, and remembered that his one remaining earthly duty was to die.

"It is God's will that I should die," said he at last, "and I feel that He will soon release me from all worldly cares and sufferings; but you, Mademoiselle, have made the last moments of my life happy," and again he was silent for a minute or two, while he strove to find both courage and words to express that which he wished to say. "How different have been the last few weeks of my existence since first I was allowed to look upon your face!" A faint blush suffused Agatha's brow as Cathelineau spoke. "Yes, Mademoiselle," he continued, "I know you will forgive, when coming from a dying man, words which would have been insane had they been spoken at any other time—my life has been wholly different since that day when your brother led me, unwilling as I was, into your presence at Durbellière. Since that time I have had no other thought than of you; it was you who gave me courage in battle, and, more wonderful than that, enabled me to speak aloud, and with authority among those who were all so infinitely my superiors. It was your beauty that softened my rough heart, your spirit that made me dauntless, your influence that raised me up so high. I have not dared to love you as love is usually described, for they say that love without hope makes the heart miserable, and my thoughts of you have made me more blessed than I ever was before, and yet I hoped for nothing; but I have adored you as I hardly dared to adore anything that was only human. I hardly know why I should have had myself carried hither to tell you this, but I felt that I should die more easily, when I had confessed to you the liberty which my thoughts had taken with your image."

As he continued speaking, Agatha had risen from her seat, and she was now kneeling at the foot of his bed, hiding her face between her hands, and the tears were streaming fast down her cheeks.

"Tell me, Mademoiselle, that you forgive me," said he, "tell me that you pardon my love, and above all, pardon me for speaking of it. I have now but a few hours' breath, and in them I feel that I shall be but feeble; but tell me that you forgive me, and, though dying, I shall be happy."

Agatha was too agitated to speak for a time, but she stretched her hand out to him, and he grasped it in his own as forcibly as his strength would allow.

"I know that you have pardoned my boldness," said he. "May God bless you, and protect you in the dangers which are coming."

"May He bless you also, Cathelineau—dear Cathelineau," said Agatha, still sobbing. "May He bless you, and receive you into His glory, and seat you among His angels, and make you blessed and happy in His presence for ever and ever through eternity." And she drew herself nearer to him, and kissed the hand which she still held within her own, and bathed it with her tears, and pressed it again and again to her bosom. "The memory of the words you have spoken to me shall be dearer to me than the love of man, shall be more precious to me than any homage a living prince could lay at my feet—to remember that Cathelineau has loved me—that the sainted Cathelineau has held my image in his heart, shall be love enough for Agatha Larochejaquelin."

Cathelineau lingered on for the whole of that day, and the greater portion of the night. Agatha did not leave his bed-side for a moment, but sat during most of the time still holding his hand in hers. He spoke no farther respecting the singular passion he had nursed in his heart, nor did she allude to it; but when he spoke at all, he felt that he was speaking to a dear, and tried, and valued friend, and he spoke, therefore, without hesitation and without reserve. He desired her to give various messages from him to the Vendean chiefs, but especially to de Lescure, to whom he said he looked with most hope for a successful issue to the struggle. He begged that they might be told that his last breath was spent in advising that they should make one great, combined, and final effort for the total overthrow of republicanism in France, and not fritter away their strength in prolonged contests with an enemy so infinitely their superior in numbers. Agatha promised faithfully to be a true messenger of these last injunctions, and then she saw the Vendean chief expire in perfect tranquillity, happy in an assured hope of everlasting joy.

He died about three in the morning, and before five, Henri Larochejaquelin arrived at St. Laurent from Clisson. He had ridden hard through the previous day and the entire night, with the hope of once more seeing the leader, whom he had followed with so much devotion, and valued so truly; but he was too late.

He caught his sister in his arms as he ran up the hospital stairs. "Where is he?" said he; "is he still alive? Is there any hope?"

"There is no hope for us," answered Agatha; "but there is perfect certainty for him. The good Cathelineau has restored his spirit to Him who gave it to avenge His glory."

CHAPTER VI
COMMISSIONERS OF THE REPUBLIC

The taking Saumur frightened the Convention much more than any of the previous victories of the Vendeans. The republicans lost a vast quantity of military stores, arms, gunpowder, cannons, and soldiers' clothing; and, which was much worse than the loss itself these treasures had fallen into the hands of an enemy, whose chief weakness consisted in the want of such articles. The royalists since the beginning of the revolt had always shewn courage and determination in action; but they had never before been collected in such numbers, or combated with forces so fully prepared for resistance, as those whom they had so signally conquered at Saumur. The Convention began to be aware that some strong effort would be necessary to quell the spirit of the Vendeans. France at the time was surrounded by hostile troops. At the moment in which the republicans were flying from the royalists at Saumur, the soldiers of the Convention were marching out of Valenciennes, that fortified city having been taken by the united arms of Austria and England. Condé also had fallen, and on the Rhine, the French troops who had occupied Mayence with so much triumph, were again on the point of being driven from it by the Prussians.

The Committee of Public Safety, then the repository of the supreme power in Paris, was aware that unless the loyalty of La Vendée was utterly exterminated, the royalists of that district would sooner or later join themselves to the allies, and become the nucleus of an overpowering aristocratic party in France. There were at the time thousands, and tens and hundreds of thousands in France who would gladly have welcomed the extinction of the fearful Republic which domineered over them, had not every man feared to express his opinion. The Republic had declared, that opposition to its behests, in deed, or in word, or even in thought, as far as thoughts could be surmised, should be punished with death; and by adhering to the purport of this horrid decree, the voice of a nation returning to its senses was subdued. Men feared to rise against the incubus which oppressed them, lest others more cowardly than themselves should not join them; and the Committee of Public Safety felt that their prolonged existence depended on their being able to perpetuate this fear. It determined, therefore, to strike terror into the nation by exhibiting a fearful example in La Vendée. After full consideration, the Committee absolutely resolved to exterminate the inhabitants of the country—utterly to destroy them all, men, women, and children—to burn every town, every village, and every house—to put an end to all life in the doomed district, and to sweep from the face of the country man, beast, and vegetable. The land was to be left without proprietors, without a population, and without produce; it was to be converted into a huge Golgotha, a burial-place for every thing that had life within it; and then, when utterly purged by fire and massacre, it was to be given up to new colonists, good children of the Republic, who should enjoy the fertility of a land soaked with the blood of its former inhabitants. Such was the deliberate resolution of the Committee of Public Safety, and no time was lost in commencing the work of destruction.

Barrère, one of the members of the Committee, undertook to see the work put in a proper train, and for this purpose he left Paris for the scene of action. Westerman and Santerre accompanied him, and to them was committed the task of accomplishing the wishes of the Committee. There was already a republican army in La Vendée, under the command of General Biron, but the troops of which it was composed were chiefly raw levies, recruits lately collected by the conscription, without discipline, and, in a great degree, without courage; but the men who were now brought to carry on the war, were the best soldiers whom France could supply. Westerman brought with him a legion of German mercenaries, on whom he could rely for the perpetration of any atrocity, and Santerre was at the head of the seven thousand men, whom the allied army had permitted to march out of Valenciennes, and to return to Paris.

It was in the beginning of July that this worthy triumvirate met at Angers, on their road to La Vendée. Cathelineau had driven the republican garrison out of this town immediately after the victory at Saumur, but the royalists made no attempt to keep possession of it, and the troops who had evacuated it at their approach, returned to it almost immediately. It was now thronged with republican soldiers of all denominations, who exercised every species of tyranny over the townspeople. Food, drink, forage, clothes, and even luxuries were demanded, and taken in the name of the Convention from every shop, and the slightest resistance to these requisitions, was punished as treason to the Republic. The Vendeans, in possession of the same town only a fortnight before, had injured no one, had taken nothing without paying for it, aid had done everything to prevent the presence of their army being felt as a curse; and yet Angers was a noted republican town; it had shown no favours to the royalists, and received with open arms the messengers of the Convention. Such was the way in which the republicans rewarded their friends, and the royalists avenged themselves on their enemies.

One hot July evening, five men were seated in a parlour of the Mayor's house in Angers, but the poor Mayor himself was not allowed, nor probably did he wish, to be one of the party. Glasses were on the table before them, and the empty bottles, which were there also, showed, that however important the subjects might be which they were discussing, they still considered that some degree of self-indulgence was compatible with their duties. The air of the room was heavy with tobacco smoke, and one or two of the number still had cigars between their lips. They were all armed, though two of them were not in uniform, and the manner in which they had their arms disposed, showed that they did not quite conceive themselves to be in security in these their convivial moments. The men were Barrère, Westerman, and Santerre, and two of the republican Generals, Chouardin and Bourbotte.

Westerman and the two latter were in uniform, and the fact of their having arms, was only in keeping with their general appearance: but the other two were in plain clothes, and their pistols, which were lying among the glasses on the table, and the huge swords which stood upright against their chairs, gave a hideous aspect to the party, and made them look as though they were suspicious of each other.

Barrère alone had no sword. His hand was constantly playing with a little double-barrelled pistol, which he continually cocked and uncocked, the fellow of which lay immediately before him. He was a tall, well built, handsome man, about thirty years of age, with straight black hair, brushed upright from his forehead; his countenance gave the idea of eagerness and impetuosity, rather than cruelty or brutality. He was, however, essentially egotistical and insincere; he was republican, not from conviction, but from prudential motives; he adhered to the throne a while, and deserted it only when he saw that it was tottering; for a time he belonged to the moderate party in the Republic, and voted with the Girondists; he gradually joined the Jacobins, as he saw that they were triumphing over their rivals, and afterwards was one of those who handed over the leaders of the Reign of Terror to the guillotine, and assisted in denouncing Robespierre and St. Just. He was one of the very few who managed to outlive the Revolution, which he did for nearly half a century.

His face was hardly to be termed prepossessing, but it certainly did not denote the ruthless ferocity which the nature of the task he had undertaken would require, and which he exercised in its accomplishment. Nature had not formed him to be a monster gloating in blood; the Republic had altered the disposition which nature had given him, and he learnt among those with whom he had associated, to delight in the work which they required at his hands. Before the Reign of Terror was over, he had become one of those who most loudly called for more blood, while blood was running in torrents on every side; it was he who demanded the murder of the Queen, when even Robespierre was willing to save her. It was he who declared in the Convention that the dead were the only enemies who never returned; and yet this same man lived to publish a pamphlet, in which he advocated the doctrine, that under no circumstances could one human being be justified in taking the life of another.

He was dressed in a blue dress-coat, which in spite of the heat of the weather, was buttoned close round his body; he was rather a dandy in his costume, for his tightly-fitted breeches were made to show the form of his well-formed leg, and his cravat was without a wrinkle. Before the Revolution, Barrère had been a wealthy aristocrat.

Santerre, who sat next to him, was in every respect unlike the ci-devant nobleman. He was a large, rough, burly man, about forty years of age; his brown hair was long and uncombed, his face was coarse and hot, and the perspiration was even now running down it, though drinking and smoking was at present his hardest work; his lips were thick and sensual, and his face was surrounded by huge whiskers, which made him look uncouth and savage; his cravat was thrown off, and his shirt was open at the neck, so as to show his brown throat and brawny chest; a huge horse pistol lay before him close to his glass, and a still huger sword stood up against his chair. He was drinking hard and talking loudly, and was evidently quite at ease with his company; he was as completely at home in the Mayor's parlour at Angers, as when rushing into the Tuilleries at the head of his fellow citizens from the faubourg St. Antoine.

Santerre was of Flemish descent, and by trade a brewer. He was possessed of considerable wealth, which he freely spent among the poor, while famine pressed sore upon them; he was consequently loved, followed, and obeyed. He was the King of the Faubourgs; and though the most ruthless in his animosity to the royalists, he was not altogether a bad man, neither was he by nature absolutely cruel. He had adopted the Revolution from a belief that the great mass of the people would be better off in the world without kings, nobility, or aristocrats; and having made himself firm in this belief, he used to the utmost his coarse, huge, burly power in upsetting these encumbrances on the nation. His love of liberty had become a fanaticism. He had gone with the current, and he had no fine feelings to be distressed at the horrid work which he had to do, no humanity to be shocked; but he was not one of those who delighted in bloodshed and revelled in the tortures which he inflicted on others. He had been low in the world's esteem, and the Revolution had raised him to a degree of eminence; this gratified his ambition, and made him a ready tool in the hands of those who knew how to use his well-known popularity, his wealth, his coarse courage and great physical powers.

Westerman sat at the window a little away from the others. He was a man of indomitable courage and undying perseverance. He was a German, who had been banished from Prussia, and having entered the French army as a private soldier had gradually risen to be an officer. A short time before the storming of the Tuilleries he had foreseen that the democratic party was prevailing, and he had joined it. Danton and Santerre had discovered and appreciated his courage and energy, and he soon found himself a leader of the people. It was he who directed the movements of the populace on the 10th of August, when the Tuilleries was sacked, and the Swiss guards were massacred on the steps of the King's palace. Since that time Westerman had been a successful soldier in the republican army, not that he was by any means a vehement democrat: his object had been military success, and that only. He had neither political theories or political ambition. Chance had thrown him in the way of the Republic, and he had become a republican. He was then attached to the army of Dumourier as aide-de-camp to that General, and was in the confidence of him and of Danton, at the moment that Dumourier was endeavouring to hand over the armies of the Republic to the power of Prussia and of Austria. He again, however, was wise in time. Dumourier calculated too entirely on the affection of the army to himself and failed; but before he failed, Westerman had left him. He was now again a trustworthy servant of the Republic, and as such was sent to assist in the fearful work which the tyranny of the democrats required.

His unnatural ruthlessness and prompt obedience were of no avail to him. Soon after his return from the western provinces he perished under the guillotine.

"And so the good Cathelineau is dead," said Santerre. "The invincible, the invulnerable, the saint! ha, ha! What sweet names these dear friends of ours have given themselves."

"Yes," said General Bourbotte; "the messenger who told me had come direct from their hospital; Cathelineau breathed his last the day before yesterday at St. Laurent."

"Let us drink to his health, gentlemen; his spiritual health," said Santerre; "and to his safe journey;" and the brewer raised his glass to his lips, and drank the toast which he had proposed.

"Bon voyage, my dear Cathelineau," said Bourbotte, following his example.

"Cathelineau was a brave man," said Chouardin. "I am glad he died of his wounds; I should have been sorry that so gallant a fellow should have had to submit his neck to the sharp embraces of Mademoiselle Guillotine."

"That is hardly a patriotic sentiment, citizen General," said Barrère. "Gallantry on the part of an insurgent royalist is an inspiration of the devil, sent to induce man to perpetuate the degradation and misery of his fellow-men. Such gallantry, or rather such frenzy, should give rise to anything but admiration in the breast of a patriot."

"My fidelity to the Republic will not be doubted, I believe," said Chouardin, "because, as a soldier, I admire high courage when I find it in a soldier."

"If your fidelity be unimpeachable, your utility will be much questioned, if you wish to spare a royalist because he is a brave man," said Barrère. "By the same argument, I presume, you would refrain from knocking an adder on the head, because he rose boldly in your path."

"Who talked of sparing?" said Chouardin. "I only said that I would sooner that a brave enemy should die in battle than be handled by an executioner. Talk as you will, you cannot disgrace such a man as Cathelineau."

"Cannot I, indeed, citizen General?" said Westerman, rising from his seat and coming into the middle of the room. "I do then utterly despise, scorn, and abominate him, and all such as him. I can conceive nothing in human form more deplorably low, more pitiably degraded, than such a poor subservient slave as he was."

"There, Westerman, you are grossly wrong," said Santerre. "Your cowardly Marquis, run-fling from the throne which he pretends to reverence, but does not dare to protect; whose grand robes and courtly language alone have made him great; who has not heart enough even to love the gay puppets who have always surrounded him, or courage enough to fight for the unholy wealth he has amassed: this man I say is contemptible. Such creatures are as noxious vermin, whom one loathes, and loathing them destroys. You no less destroy the tiger, who ravages the green fields which your labour has adorned; who laps the blood of your flocks, and threatens the life of your children and servants, but you do not despise the tiger; you keep his hide, as a monument of your victory over a brave and powerful enemy. Cathelineau was the tiger, who was destroying, before it had ripened, the precious fruit of the Revolution."

"The tiger is a noble beast," said Westerman. "He is hungry, and he seeks his prey; he is satisfied, and he lays down and sleeps; but Cathelineau was a mean jackal, who strove for others, not for himself. I can understand the factious enmity of the born aristocrat, who is now called upon to give up the titles, dignities, and so-called honours, which, though stolen from the people, he has been taught to look upon as his right. He contends for a palpable possession which his hand has grasped, which he has tasted and long enjoyed. I know that he is a robber and a spoiler of the poor; I know, in short, that he is an aristocrat, and as such I would have him annihilated, abolished from the face of the earth. I would that the aristocrats of France had but one neck, that with a grasp of my own hand, I might at once choke out their pernicious breath," and the republican laid upon the table his huge hand, and tightly clenched his fingers as though he held between them the imaginary throat of the aristocracy of France; "but," continued he, "much as I hate a gentleman, ten times more strongly do I hate, despise, and abhor the subservient crew of spiritless slaves who uphold the power of the masters, who domineer over them, who will not accept the sweet gift of liberty, who are kicked, and trodden on, and spat upon, and will not turn again; who will not rise against their tyrants, even when the means of doing so are brought to their hands; who willingly, nay, enthusiastically, lay their necks in the dust, that their fellow-creatures may put their feet upon them. Of such was this Cathelineau, and of such I understand are most of those who hound on these wretched peasants to sure destruction. For them I have no pity, and with them I have no sympathy. They have not the spirit of men, and I would rejoice that the dogs should lick their blood from off the walls, and that birds of prey should consume their flesh."

"Westerman is right," said Barrère; "they are mean curs, these Vendeans, and like curs they must be destroyed; the earth must be rid of men who know not how to take possession of their property in that earth which nature has given them. Believe me, citizen General, that any sympathy with such a reptile as Cathelineau is not compatible with the feeling which should animate the heart of a true republican, intending honestly and zealously to do the work of the Republic."

General Chouardin made no reply to the rebuke which these words conveyed; he did not dare to do so; he did not dare to repeat the opinion that there was anything admirable in the courage of a royalist. Much less than had now been said had before this been deemed sufficient to mark as a victim for the revolutionary tribunal some servant of the Republic, and few wished to experience the tender mercies of Fouquier Tinville, the public accuser. Even Santerre was silenced; despite his popularity, his well-known devotion to the cause, his hatred of the aristocrats, and his aversion to royalty, so horridly displayed at the execution of the King, even he felt that it might not be safe for him to urge that the memory of Cathelineau was not despicable.

"His death must have much weakened them," said Bourbotte. "I know them well, the miscreants! I doubt if they will follow any other leader, that is, in great numbers. The fools looked on this man as a kind of god; they now find that their god is dead. I doubt whether there is another leader among them, who can induce them to leave their parishes."

"If they won't come to us," said Barrère, "we must go to them; they have gone too far now to recede. Whether they return to their homes, or again take up arms, matters little; they must all be destroyed, for blood alone can establish the Republic on a basis which can never be overturned."

"The name of a royalist shall be as horrible in men's ears as that of a parricide," said Santerre.

"But what will you do if you find no army to oppose you?" said Bourbotte. "You cannot well fight without an enemy."

"Never fear," said Westerman, "your muskets shall not grow rusty for want of use. We will go from parish to parish, and leave behind us dead corpses, and burning houses."

"You will not ask soldiers to do the work of executioners?" said Bourbotte.

"I expect the soldiers to do the work of the Convention," said Barrère; "and I also expect the officers to do the same: these are not times in which a man can be chary as to the work which he does."

"We must not leave a royalist alive in the west of France," said Westerman. "You may be assured, Generals, that our soldiers will obey us, however slow yours may be to obey you."

"Perhaps so," said Bourbotte; "my men have not yet been taught to massacre unarmed crowds."

"It is difficult to know what they have been taught," said Westerman. "Whenever they have encountered a few peasants with clubs in their hands, your doughty heroes have invariably ran away."

Westerman as he spoke, stood leaning on the back of a chair, and Bourbotte also rose as he answered him.

"I have yet to learn," aid he, "that you yourself ever were able to make good soldiers out of country clowns in less than a month's time.

When you have done so, then you may speak to me on the subject without impertinence."

"I give you my word, citizen General," answered Westerman, "I shall say to you, then and now, whatever I, in the performance of my duty, may think fits and if you deem me impertinent, you may settle that point with the Convention, or, if you prefer it, with myself."

"Westerman, you are unfair to General Bourbotte," said Santerre; "he has said nothing which need offend you."

"It is the General that is offended, not I," said Westerman; "I only beg that he may not talk mawkish nonsense, and tell us that his fellows are too valiant, and too noble to put to the sword unarmed royalists, when everybody knows they are good for nothing else, and that they would run and scatter from the fire of a few muskets, like a lot of plovers from a volley of stones."

"I grant you," said Bourbotte, "that my soldiers are men and not monsters. They are, as yet, French peasants, not German cut-throats."

"Now, by Heaven, Bourbotte," said the Prussian, "you shall swallow that word," and he seized a pistol from off the table. "German cut-throat! and that from you who have no other qualities of a soldier than what are to be found in a light pair of heels. You shall, at any rate, have to deal with one German, whether he be a cut-throat or not."

"In any way you please," said Bourbotte, "that is, in any open or honest way." And as he spoke, he stepped back one step, and took his sword out of the scabbard.

The pistol which Westerman had taken from the table belonged to Santerre, and when he saw it in the hand of his friend, he leapt up and seized hold of the German's arm.

"Are you mad Westerman," said he; "do you wish to fight here in the Mayor's house? I tell you, you were wrong, in taunting him as you did; sit quiet till I make peace between you."

"Taunting him! now, by Heaven, that is good. I will leave it to Barrère to say who first taunted the other. Nonsense, Santerre, leave hold of me I say: you do not think I am going to murder the man, do you?"

General Chouardin also got up and put himself between the two armed men. "Put up your sword, Bourbotte," whispered he, leading him off to the further window of the room; "you are no match for him here: if Barrère chooses he will have you recalled to Paris, and your neck will then not be worth a month's purchase."

"Gentlemen," said Barrère, "this will never do. You can neither of you serve the nation well if you persist in quarrelling between yourselves. General Bourbotte, you should apologize to our friend Westerman for the insult which you offered to his countrymen."

"My country is the country of my adoption," said Westerman. "I ceased to be a German when I took up the arms of France; but my soldiers are my children, and an insult to them is an injury to myself."

"If your anger can wait till the revolt in La Vendée has been quelled," said Chouardin, "my friend Bourbotte will be ready enough to satisfy your wishes as a citizen. Barrère truly says, this is no time for private quarrels."

"So be it," said Westerman. "Let General Bourbotte remember that he owes me an apology or redress."

"You shall have any redress, which any arms you may be pleased to name can give you," said Bourbotte.

"By my honour then, you are two fools," said Santerre; "two egregious fools, if you cannot at once forget the angry words which you each have used. Have your own way, however, so long as you do not fight here."

As the brewer was yet speaking, a servant knocked at the door, and said that a young man wished to say a few words to citizen Santerre on especial business, and on the service of the Republic.

"On the service of the Republic?" said Santerre. "Show him in here then; I have no official secrets from my colleagues."

The servant, however, stated that the young man would not make his appearance in the room where the party were sitting, and he declared he would go away if he could not see Santerre alone. The republican at length yielded, and followed the servant into a small sitting-room, where he found our friend, Adolphe Denot.

CHAPTER VII
BATTLE OF AMAILLOU

It will be remembered that Adolphe Denot left the council-room of the royalist leaders at Saumur in anger; and that, after a few words with Henri Larochejaquelin, departed no one knew whither, or for what purpose. On leaving Henri in the street, he had himself no fixed resolve as to his future conduct; he was only determined no longer to remain leagued with men, among whom he felt himself to be disgraced. De Lescure had seen him hesitate in the hour of danger, and had encouraged him in vain; he knew that after this he could never again bear to meet the calm grey eye of his friend's cousin; he had not only been not selected as one of the Generals, but he had even been rejected, and that by the very man who had seen his cowardice. His love, moreover, had been refused by Agatha, and he deemed this refusal an injury which demanded vengeance from his hands; from the moment in which he left her room in Durbellière, schemes had floated across his half-bewildered brain for the accomplishment of his object. He still loved Agatha, though his love was, as it were, mingled with hatred; he still wished to possess her, but he did not care how disagreeable, how horrible to herself might be the means by which he accomplished his object. He entertained ideas of seizing upon her person, taking her from Durbellière, and marrying her during the confusion which the Revolution had caused in the country. At first he had no distinct idea of treachery towards the royalists with whom he had sided; though vague thoughts of bringing the soldiers of the Convention to Durbellière, in the dead of night, had at different times entered his mind, he had never reduced such thoughs to a palpable plan, nor had he ever endeavoured to excuse to himself the iniquity of such a scheme, as a man does when he resolves to sacrifice his honour and his honesty to his passions.

It was in the council-room at Saumur that he first felt a desire to betray the friends of his life; it was in the moment of his hot anger, after leaving it, that he determined to put into effect the plan which he had already conceived; it was then that insane ambition and selfish love prompted him to forget every feeling which he had hitherto recognized as honourable, and to commit himself to a deed which would make it impossible that he should ever be reconciled with the companions of his youth. He had no presentiment that he should ever rise to honour or distinction in the army of the Republic; he never even thought of what his future life would be: revenge was his object, and the sweet delight of proving to Agatha Larochejaquelin that he was able to carry out the bold threats, which he knew that she had scorned and derided.

It would be too much to say that Adolphe Denot was insane, for that would imply that he was not responsible for his own actions; but there certainly lacked something in his brain or mind, which is necessary to perfect sanity. He was no fool; he had read, enjoyed, and perhaps written poetry; he was, for the times, well educated; he could talk fluently, and, occasionally, even persuasively; he understood rapidly, and perceived correctly, the arguments and motives of others; but he could not regulate his conduct, either from the lessons he had learnt from books, or from the doings or misdoings of those around him. He wished to be popular, powerful and distinguished, but he was utterly ignorant of the means by which men gain the affection, respect, and admiration of their fellow-men; he possessed talent without judgment, and ambition without principle. As a precocious boy, he had been too much admired; he had assumed at an early age the duty of a man, and had at once been found miserably wanting.

On leaving Henri in the streets of Saumur, he went to his lodging, took with him what money he had, got upon his horse, and rode out of the town by the temporary bridge which had been put up for the transit of the shaved prisoners. He had wandered about the country for three weeks, remaining sometimes in one place, and sometimes in another, endeavouring to mature his plans; and hearing of the arrival of Santerre in Augers, had come thither to offer his services to the republicans, in the invasion which he understood they contemplated making into the Bocage.

His appearance was not very attractive when first he introduced himself to the republican, for he was lean with anxiety and worn with care; his eyes were restless and bloodshot, and his limbs trembled beneath him. Santerre was not a man who much regarded externals; but, as he afterwards said, "he did not much like the hang-dog look of the royalist cur."

Denot, in an awkward way, got through his story; he had been one of the insurgent Vendeans, he said, but he now wished to serve the Republic. He was intimately acquainted with the royalist leaders, especially the two most popular of them, de Lescure and Larochejaquelin. He knew and was willing to betray their plans. He would accompany Santerre to the residences of these Vendean Generals, and undertake to give them, their families, and possessions, into the power of the republicans, and for these services he asked but one favour; that he should be present at the contemplated burning of Durbellière, and be allowed to save the life of one female who resided there. He represented that his animosity arose entirely from the rejection of his love, and that his only object was to carry off the sister of the Vendean chief from the burning ashes of her father's château.

"Are you aware, young man," said Santerre, with something of generosity in the warning which he gave—a generosity probably inspired by the wine he had drunk: "are you aware, that should I agree to your proposal, every other member of her family will be put to death before your eyes —her brother, her old father, and every pestilent royalist we may find about the place?"

"I suppose they will," said Denot moodily. "At any rate, they deserve no protection at my hands."

"You have probably eaten their bread and drank their wine. You say, indeed, you have lived long in this rambling château, and have fought side by side with this hot-headed young brigand. Bethink you, my friend, you are angry now, but it may turn your stomach, when you are cool, to see the blood of those you know so well running like water; besides, you are taking but an unlikely road to the heart of the girl you say you love. No one has heard your plot but myself: I advise you to abandon it; if you do so, I will forget that I have heard it. You are angry now; go home and sleep on it."

"Sleep on it! I have slept on it these three weeks. No, I did not come to you till I was fully resolved. As for these people, I owe them nothing; they have scorned and rejected me; and as for the girl's heart, it is not that I seek now. Let me gain her person, and her heart will follow. A woman soon learns to love him whom she is forced to obey."

"Well, be it as you will," said Santerre. "It is all a matter of taste; only remember, that before I accede to your proposal, I must consult with my colleagues in the next room, and that when once I have spoken to them it will be too late for me to go back."

Denot declared that he had formed his resolution after mature consideration, and that he was ready and willing to carry through the work he had proposed for himself; and Santerre, without making any further objection, rejoined his friends in the next room, and explained to them the offer which had been made to him. Barrère at first opposed any treaty with Denot. He recommended that the young man should be kept as a prisoner, and at once handed over to the revolutionary tribunal.

"What good can he do us?" said he; "we can find our way to this Durbellière without his assistance; let him and the girl he wishes to kidnap pay the penalty of their crimes against the Republic. She is, I suppose, one of those modern Joans of Arc, who inspire the flagging spirits of these peasants. Should she have beauty enough to make her worth preserving, let her be the prize of some true republican. As for him, let him stretch his neck beneath the guillotine."

Barrère, however, was overruled. The Generals who were with him knew too well the nature of the country they were about to invade, not to appreciate the value of such a guide as they might find in Denot: a guide, who not only knew the nature of the country they had to traverse, and the position of the places they wished to attack, but who was also intimate with the insurgent chiefs, acquainted with their persons and their plans, and who would probably disclose, under proper management, every secret of the revolt. It was accordingly agreed that his offer should be accepted, and he was introduced by Santerre to his four confederates.

"Sit down, my friend," said Barrère, "sit down. Our colleague here informs us that you are sick of these mawkish royalists, and are willing to serve the Republic. Is it so, young man?"

"I have told M. Santerre—" said Denot. "Citizen Santerre, if you please," said Barrère; "or General Santerre, if you like it better. Monsieur and Monseigneur are a little out of fashion just at present on this side of the Loire."

"As they soon also shall be on the other," said Westerman.

"Well, I have told him," and Denot pointed to Santerre, "what it is I propose to do for you, and the terms on which I will do it."

"Terms indeed!" said Barrère. "The Republic is not accustomed to make terms with her servants. Come, tell us at once: are you a republican?"

Denot hesitated; not that he was ashamed to own himself a republican, but his blood was boiling with passion at the language and tone in which he was addressed, and yet he did not dare to shew his anger.

"Of course he is a republican," said Santerre, "or why would he come here? Take a glass of wine, friend Denot, and pluck up your courage," and Santerre passed the wine-bottle to him. "If you are true to us, you need not fear us."

"He must pronounce himself a republican," said Barrère, "or we cannot deal with him. Come, young man, can you put your mouth to so much inconvenience as to give us some slight inkling of your present political principles? All we know of you as yet is, that three weeks since you were a pestilent royalist, and a leader of royalists."

"I am a republican," said Denot.

"The Republic is made happy by your adhesion," said Barrère, bowing to him with mock solemnity across the table.

"What surety do you mean to offer us, citizen Denot," said Westerman, "that you are acting with us in good faith?"

"Do I not give you my life?" said Denot. "What other surety can I give, or can you require? What am I, or what are the royalists to gain by my proving false?"

"You say truly," answered Westerman; "you give us your life as a surety for your good faith to us. You may be assured that we will exact the penalty, if we have the slightest suspicion of foul play."

Denot made no answer, and he was questioned no further. The party soon after broke up, and the young deserter was handed over to the care of one of Santerre's sub-officers, with injunctions that he should be well and civilly treated, but that he should not be allowed to go abroad by himself; in fact, he was to be regarded as a prisoner.

"Do not be disheartened," said Santerre to him. "You can understand that under the circumstances, such precautions must be necessary. The day after tomorrow we start on our march, and you shall ride close to myself. When Clisson and Durbellière are in ashes, you shall be free to take your own course; in the meantime, no indignity shall be offered to you."

On the day named by Santerre, the whole republican army started from Angers, and commenced their march towards the Bocage. They proceeded on their route for several days without finding any enemy to contend with. They kept on the northern shore of the Loire till they reached Saumur, where they remained a couple of days, and employed themselves in punishing the inhabitants in whose houses the leaders of the Vendeans had been entertained. It was in vain that these poor men pleaded that they had not even opened their doors to the royalists till after the republican General had capitulated; that they had given nothing which they had been able to refuse, and, in fact, that they had only sold their goods and let their rooms to the Vendeans, when they could not possibly have declined to do so. Their arguments were of no avail; they were thrown into prison as criminals, and left for trial by the revolutionary tribunal.

Although Saumur had so lately been besieged and taken by the royalists, there was hardly a vestige of the conquerors left in it. Their attempt to place a garrison in the town had proved entirely a failure; the peasants who had undertaken the work had left the place by scores at a time, and before a fortnight was over, the commandant found himself with about twenty-five men, and consequently he marched back into La Vendée after his army. The town was perfectly tranquil when the republicans entered it, but the citizens were afflicted and out of spirits; their shops were closed, and their goods hidden; the bakers had no bread, the butchers no meat, and the grocers had neither oil nor sugar. They knew well what it was to sell their merchandise to the troops of the Convention, and to be paid for them by the government in assignats.

Many of those who had formed the former garrison of Saumur, were now with the army; men whom Chapeau and his assistants had shaven, men still bald, and smarting from the indignity to which they had been subjected. They wreaked their vengeance on the scene of their disgrace, and on all those who had in any way lent, or were suspected to have lent, their aid to its consummation. The furniture of the Town-hall was broken in pieces; the barbers' shops were ransacked, and their razors, brushes, and basins scattered through the street; nor was this the worst; one poor wretch was recognized who had himself wielded a razor on the occasion; he was dragged from his little shop by those on whom he had operated, and was swung up by his neck from a lamp-iron in the sight of his wife and children, who had followed his persecutors through the street. The poor woman pleaded on her knees for the life of her husband, as a wife can plead for the life of him whom she loves better than the whole world. She offered all her little wealth and her prayers; she supplicated them with tears and with blessings; she seized hold of the knees of the wretch who held the rope, and implored him by his remembrance of his father, by his regard for his own wife, his love for his own children, to spare to her the father of her infants; but she asked in vain; the man, feeling that his legs were encumbered, spurned the woman from him with his foot, and kept his hand tight upon the lamp-rope till the dying convulsions of the poor barber had ceased.

No notice was taken by the republican Generals of this murder; at any rate no punishment followed it; the next morning the army resumed its march, and left the town hated, cursed, feared, and yet obeyed. The people were now royalists in their hearts, but they did not dare to express their feelings even in whispers to each other, so frightful to them was the vengeance of the Republic. There was much policy in the fearful cruelty of the Jacobins; it was the only means by which they could have retained their power for a month.

The republicans marched on from Saumur to Montreuil, and from Montreuil to Thouars, and still found no one in arms to oppose them. Here they separated; a small party, headed by Santerre and Denot, penetrated at once from Thouars into the Bocage, and made for the château of Durbellière. It was believed that both de Lescure and Larochejaquelin were there, and Santerre expected that by hurrying across the country with a small force, he would be able to take them both and burn the château, and afterwards rejoin Westerman at Chatillon. Barrère, whose duties were not strictly those of a soldier, had not accompanied the army beyond Saumur. Westerman and the main body of the army still continued southward till they reached Parthenay, from which place it was his intention to proceed through the revolted district, burning every village; utterly destroying the towns which had not proved themselves devoted to the Republic, and slaughtering the peasants, their wives, and children wherever he could find them.

The Vendeans had not yet sufficiently matured their plans to enable them to encounter successfully the republican army. The death of Cathelineau had had a great effect upon the peasants: those who were with him had returned home in sorrow and despair, and this feeling was general, even among those who had not been at Nantes. De Lescure and Henri, however, had not despaired; after having seen the body of his General consigned to the dust, Henri had returned to Clisson, and he and his cousin were again busy in raising recruits, or rather in collecting their men, when they heard that Westerman, with an enormous army, was marching into Parthenay, and that it was his intention to proceed from thence into the Bocage, by way of Amaillou and Bressuire.

They had hardly heard this report, when the little village of Amaillou was on fire; it was the first place that was utterly burnt down, and laid in ashes by the republicans; not a house was left standing, or hardly the ruined wall of a house. The church itself was set on fire and burnt, with its pictures, its altars, and all its sacred treasures; the peasants ran from the ruins, carrying with them their wives and children, the old, the crippled, and infirm: hundreds were left dead and dying among the smoking ashes. This feat having been accomplished, Westerman continued on towards Bressuire, intending to burn the château at Clisson, as he passed it on his way.

The district between Amaillou and Bressuire is thickly studded with trees. The roads, or rather lanes, are all lined by avenues of limes and beeches. The fields are small, and surrounded by lofty hedges, which are also, in a great measure, composed of large trees, and the whole country in July, when the foliage is at the thickest, has almost the aspect of one continued forest.

Westerman had obtained guides to show him the road to Clisson. It was about six o'clock in the evening when the advanced portion of his army, consisting of three thousand men, had proceeded about a league from Amaillou. He was himself riding nearly at the front of the column, talking to his aide-de-camp and one of the guides, when he was startled by hearing a noise as of disturbed branches in the hedge, only a few feet in advance of the spot in which he was standing; he had not, however, time to give an order, or speak a word on the subject, before a long sudden gleam of fire flashed before his eyes; it was so near to him that it almost blinded him: a cannon had been fired off close to his face, and it was easy to track the fatal course of the ball; it had been directed right along the road, and was glutted with carnage before its strength was spent.

Nor did the cannon shot come alone: a fearful fire from about five hundred muskets was poured from the hedge on either side, directly into the road: the assailants were within a few feet of their enemy at the moment they were firing, and every shot took effect. Out of the four hundred men who headed the column, above half were killed, or so badly wounded as to be incapable of motion. The narrow lane, for it was no more than a lane, was nearly blocked up with carcases. Westerman, who was possessed of a courage that was never shaken, was nevertheless so thunderstruck, that he knew not what orders to give. The republicans at the head of the column, who had not themselves been struck, fired their fusils into the hedges, but their fire did no injury; it was all lost among the leaves, for the men who had attacked them were kneeling on their knees or lying on their bellies, and in the confusion which they had occasioned, were reloading their muskets.

The guide and the aide-de-camp to whom Westerman was speaking, had both fallen, and the horse upon which he himself was riding was so badly wounded, as to be unmanageable. He got off, and ran along under the hedge till he met an officer. "Give me your horse, Gerard," said he; "but no, stay where you are, gallop back, and tell Bourbotte to bring up the men. Quick, mind—so quick, that they can neither see nor hear what has happened. Bid him force his way through the hedge to the right, when he gets to the corner."

The young officer turned quickly to obey the command of his General, and had already put his spur to the horse's flank, when another broad flash of light streamed through the hedge on the left, and the horseman and horse fell to the ground, and were mingled with a heap of wounded and dying. Young Gerard did not live long enough to be conscious of the blow which killed him. Another volley of musketry followed the cannon shot, and hardly left a man standing of those who had been the foremost. The attack had taken place so quickly, that the Vendeans had not yet had time to load again; but one of two cannons had been kept as a reserve, and about a hundred muskets had not been fired till de Lescure gave the word of command. The first attack was made under the direction of Henri Larochejaquelin.

Westerman was standing between the hedge and the mounted officer, when the latter fell with his horse, and the blood from the poor animal nearly covered him from head to foot. "Into the field, my men," said he to those who were near enough to hear him; "follow me through the hedge," and with a considerable effort he forced his way through the underwood, and he was followed and accompanied by all those who were still standing near him; but when he got there, not one of the Vendeans was to be seen; there were traces enough of them in the grass, and among the broken boughs, but the men had retreated after the first fire, and were now again lying in ambush behind the next hedge.

In about five minutes, there were two or three hundred republicans in the fields to the right of the road, for the army was still advancing; but they did not know where to go or what to do. They were looking about for an enemy, and in dread of being fired on, not only from the hedges, but even out of the trees. Westerman, however, got the men formed into some kind of order, and bid them advance; they did so, and on coming near to the second hedge, received another murderous fire, for every royalist had now had time to reload.

The combat continued for some time, for the republicans contrived to make their way into the second field; but the royalists again sheltered themselves behind the further hedge, and repeated their fire from their lurking-place. It was in vain that the republicans fired into the hedges; their shot either passed over the heads of the Vendeans, or were lost among the roots and trunks of the trees. Every one of the royalists, on the other hand fired, with a clear aim, and almost invariably with deadly effect. Westerman felt that it would be useless to pursue them; his soldiers, moreover, were already flying without orders. He had not the least idea what was the number of the enemy with whom he was engaged, what was their means of carrying on the battle, or on what side of him the greater number of them were situated; he therefore determined to retreat, and led back the whole of his army over the still burning ashes of the miserable village which he had destroyed that morning. The greater portion of the men were forced to go back as far as Parthenay, but he himself remained with a small detachment in the neighbourhood of Amaillou. He was determined, if possible, to be revenged that same night for the defeat which he had experienced.

The two cousins were at Clisson when they first heard that Westerman was actually on his road towards Bressuire, and they had lost no time in taking the best measures in their power to stop his progress, but they had not even hoped that their effort would have been so successful as it proved. The tocsin had been rung in the three neighbouring parishes, and about seven hundred men had been collected. These men all possessed muskets, but they themselves had no ammunition, and the whole supply which could be found in the district, including the little depot at Clisson, only sufficed to give the men some three and some four rounds each. When Westerman, with his ten thousand men, retreated from about seven hundred, the royalists had not one charge of powder to three muskets among them.

About ten in the evening Henri and de Lescure returned on foot from the battle to the château of Clisson. Henri still had the red scarf round his neck and waist, and stuck in the latter he had three or four pistols, of various sizes, all of which had been used in the recent engagement. On his shoulder he held a rifle, which he carried like a fowling-piece, and he walked home with the air and look of a man returning from a day's sport, well contented with the execution he had done.

Not so de Lescure: he was thoughtful, if not sad; and though he would not, either by a tone or a look, rebuke the gaiety of his companion, it was very evident that he did not share it. The peasants returned along the road, hurrying to their homes, shouting with glee and full of triumph. As they passed their leaders, they cheered the darling heroes who had led them to another victory, and would, had they been allowed to do so, have carried them home upon their shoulders. They had no thoughts of any further battle, or of future bloodshed and misery. They had been victorious over the blues, and that was sufficient for the present evening. They were able to return home and tell their wives and sweethearts of their triumph, and that without any drawback from friends lost or wounded. In all their contests, the Vendeans had never been victorious with so few calamities to themselves.

"I saw Westerman himself," said Henri to his friend. "I am sure I did, and what's more I was within pistol shot of him, but I hadn't a pistol loaded at the moment, or I would have put an end to his career. I wonder how he likes his reception in the Bocage."

"He is not the man to be easily daunted," said de Lescure. "You'll find it will not be long before he advances again. If he were to march to Bressuire tomorrow, what is to stop him?"

"Why not stop him tomorrow as we have done today?" said Henri.

"The men are all gone home," said the other.

"They will all assemble again tomorrow," said Henri; "we have only to have the bells rung at seven o'clock, or six, or five, or when you will, and you will find that every man will be ready for another day's work, and that without a murmur."

"And will they bring powder with them, Henri?"

"Why, we are rather short off for powder," said he. "Our affair tonight was all very well, for the enemy lost an immense number, and we lost none; but yet it was unsatisfactory, for the fellows have left nothing behind them. I'll tell you what, Charles, we ought to follow them to Parthenay."

"Impossible," said de Lescure.

"Why impossible, Charles? Why is Parthenay, which is not better fortified than Clisson, be more unassailable than Saumur, where everything appeared to be against us?"

"We were all together then, and now we are scattered. I'll tell you what, Henri," he continued, after walking on silent for a few steps. "I'll tell you what we must do: we must leave this district altogether; we must leave it to be ravaged by fire and sword; we must leave it to Westerman, to wreak his vengeance on it, and go to Chatillon, taking with us every armed man that will follow us. We cannot stand an invasion here in the south."

"Heavens, Charles! what do you mean? Will you not stay to protect the poor wretches who are so ready to fight for us?"

"We can protect no one by staying here. We cannot hope to contend single-handed with such an army as that which was but just now advancing to Bressuire. We can have given them a check, but you know we cannot repeat the effort of this evening. D'Elbée and Stofflet are at Chatillon; your own followers are all in that vicinity. When there, we can communicate with Bonchamps and Charette. We must go to Chatillon."

"And your wife, Charles, and Marie! you will not leave them in the château?"

"If your father and Agatha will receive them, they shall go to Durbellière."

"There you are right," said Henri. "Whatever may be the danger, let us have them together; we shall then at any rate be able to feel that we know the point which is to be defended most closely."

"We will start tomorrow, Henri; tomorrow evening. May God grant that that may be time enough. Westerman cannot collect his men so as to force a march as far as Clisson tomorrow; but before a week is over, I know that the château will be a ruin."

"Will you leave the furniture?" said Henri.

"Yes," answered de Lescure; "furniture, horses, cattle, corn—everything but my wife and child. Let everything go: am I not giving it to my King?"

CHAPTER VIII
CLISSON

De Lescure had calculated wrongly with regard to Westerman's return. It was true that he could not have again put his ten thousand men in marching order, and have returned with his whole force the next day from Bressuire as far as Clisson, but Westerman himself did not go back beyond Amaillou, and he detained there with him a small detachment of mounted men, whom he had commanded at Valmy, and whom he well knew. He kept no officers but one cornet and two sergeants, and with this small force he determined, if possible, to effect that night what his army of ten thousand men had so signally failed in accomplishing.

About half a mile from Amaillou there was a large château, the owner of which had emigrated; it had been left to the care of two or three servants, who had deserted it on the approach of the republican army, and when Westerman and his small troop rode up to the front gate, they found no one either to admit them or to dispute their entrance. Here he bivouacked for an hour or two, and matured his project, which, as yet, he had communicated to no one.

He had entrusted the retreat of the army to General Bourbotte, who, in spite of their quarrel at Angers, was serving with him; and without staying even to ascertain what was the amount of loss he had sustained, or to see whether the enemy would harass the army as it retreated, he had separated from it at Amaillou, and reached the château about ten o'clock in the evening. He had with him a couple of guides, who knew the country well, and accompanied by these, he resolved to attack Clisson that night, to burn the château of M. de Lescure, and, if possible, to carry back with him to Bressuire the next morning the two Vendean chiefs, whom he knew were staying there.

Westerman understood enough of the tactics of the Vendeans to know that this was practicable, and he had the quick wit and ready hand to conceive the plan, and put it in practice: he knew that the peasants would not remain in barracks, or even assembled together during the night, if they were near enough to their own homes to reach them; he knew that they would spend the remainder of their long summer evening in drinking, dancing, and rejoicing, and that they would then sleep as though no enemy were within a hundred miles of them; he knew that nothing could induce them to take on themselves the duties of sentinels, and that there would, in all probability, be but little to oppose him in attacking Clisson that night.

Westerman first had the horses fed, and having then refreshed his men with meat, wine, and brandy, he started at two o'clock. He was distant from Clisson about three leagues, according to the measurement of the country, or a little better than seven miles. There had hardly been any darkness during the night, and as he and his troopers sallied out of the château-yard, the dawn was just breaking in the East.

"Never mind," said he to the young cornet who rode by his side; "the light will not hurt us, for we will make them hear us before they see us. We will be back as far as this before thirty men in the parish are awake. It will be best for them who sleep soundest."

"Except for those in the château, General," said the cornet: "those who sleep there will wake to a warm breakfast."

"They will never eat breakfast more, I believe and trust," said Westerman; "for I do not think that we shall be able to take the brigands alive. Their women, however, may receive some of our rough republican hospitality at Bressuire. You had better prepare your prettiest bow and your softest words, for this sister of de Lescure is, they say, a real beauty. She shall ride to Bressuire before you on your saddle-cloth, if you choose to load your arms with such a burden; but don't grow too fond of her kisses, for though she were a second Venus, the guillotine must have the disposal of her."

The cornet made no answer, but his young heart turned sick at the brutality of his companion. His breast had glowed with republican zeal at the prospect of a night attack on the two most distinguished of the royalist chiefs. The excitement of the quick ride through the night-air, the smallness of the party, the importance of the undertaking, the probable danger, and the uncertainty, had all seemed to him delightful; and the idea of rescuing a beautiful girl from the flames was more delightful than all; but the coarseness and cruelty of his General had destroyed the romance, and dissipated the illusion. He felt that he could not offer a woman his protection, that he might carry her to a scaffold.

At about two, Westerman started on his expedition. His men carried their sabres, still sheathed, in their hands, to prevent the noise which they would have made rattling against their saddles; but still their journey through the country was anything but quiet. They only rode two abreast, as the roads were too narrow to admit of more. Westerman himself and one of the guides headed the column, and the young cornet and veteran sergeant closed the rear. They went at a fast trot, and the noise of their horses' hoofs sounded loudly on the hard parched ground. In spite of their precautions, their sabres rattled, and the curbs on their bridles jingled; and the absence of all other noises made Westerman fear that their approach must be audible, even through the soundness of a peasant's sleep.

On they rode, and as they drew near to the château, Westerman put spurs to his horse, and changed his trot into a gallop; his troop of course followed his example, and as they came to the end of their journey they abandoned all precautions; each man dropped his scabbard to his side, and drew the blade; each man put his hand to his holster, and transferred his pistol to his belt, for he did not know how soon he might have to leave his saddle; each man drew the brazen clasps of his helmet tight beneath his chin, and prepared himself for action.

"These are the Clisson woods," said the guide, almost out of breath with the quickness of his motion.

"How infernally dark they make it," said Westerman, speaking to himself. "We had light enough till we got here."

"And there are the gates," said the guide. "That first entrance which is open, goes to the back of the house; a little beyond, there is another, which leads to the front; there you will find a gate, but it is merely closed with a latch."

"Craucher," said Westerman, speaking to the second sergeant, who was riding immediately behind him, "stand at the corner, and bid the men follow me at a quick trot—all of them, mind; tell Cornet Leroy that I have changed my mind," and Westerman, followed by his troop, dashed up the narrow avenue which led through the wood to the back of the house.

The château of Clisson was surrounded by large woods, through which countless paths and little roads were made in every direction for the convenience of the woodmen, and the small tumbrils which were used for bringing out the timber and faggots. These woods came close up to the farm-yard of the château, which was again divided from the house by large walled gardens, into which the back windows opened. The road up which Westerman had ridden led under the garden-wall to the farm-yard, but another road from the front, running along the gable-end of the house, communicated with it. The door used by the servants was at the side of the château, and consequently the readiest way from the public road to the servants' door, was that by which Westerman had, at the last moment, determined to force an entrance into the château.

He trotted up till he faced the garden-wall, and then turned short round to the house, and as he rode close up under the gable-end, he gave Sergeant Craucher directions to take three men and force the door; but he and the sergeant soon saw that this trouble was spared them, for the door stood wide open before them.

We will now go back to the inhabitants of the château. De Lescure and Henri had returned thither about eleven o'clock, and although their safe return, and account of the evening's victorious engagement for a while quieted the anxious fears of Marie and Madame de Lescure, those ladies by no means felt inclined to rest quietly as though all danger were removed from their pillows. They were in a dreadful alarm at the nearness of the republicans; they knew well that their ruthless enemies spared none that fell into their hands. I should belie these heroines if I said that they feared more for themselves than for those they loved so dearly, but they were not accustomed yet to the close vicinity of danger; and when they learned that a battle had been lost and won that evening, within a mile or two, in the very next parish to that in which they lived, they looked at each other, and trembling asked what next was to be done.

"You must not leave us, Charles, you must not leave us again," said Madame de Lescure to her husband; "indeed you must not leave us here." She paused a moment, and then added, with an accent of horror which she could not control, "What would become of us if these men came upon us when you were away?"

"Wherever you go, let us go with you," said Marie, forgetting in her excitement her usual maidenly reserve, and laying her little hand as she spoke upon her lover's arm; then blushing, she withdrew it, and turned to her brother.

"Do not turn from him, Marie," said her sister-in-law. "You will soon want his strong arm, and his kind, loving heart."

"Charles will not desert me, Victorine," said Marie, blushing now more beautifully than ever, for though she knew that Henri loved her, he had never absolutely told her so. "Though you are his dearest care, he will always have a hand to stretch to his poor Marie."

Before she had finished speaking, Henri held her close in his embrace. It was perhaps hardly a fitting time for him to make an avowal of his love; but lovers cannot always choose the most proper season for their confessions. He was still hot from the battle which he had fought; his hands were still black with powder; the well-known red scarf was still twisted round his belt, and held within its folds his armament of pistols. His fair, long hair was uncombed, and even entangled with his exertions. His large boots were covered with dust, and all his clothes were stained and soiled with the grass and weeds through which he had that night dragged himself more than once, in order to place himself within pistol-shot of his enemies; and yet, soiled and hot as he was, fatigued with one battle, and meditating preparations for another, there, in the presence of de Lescure and his wife, he clasped Marie to his manly heart, and swore to her that his chief anxiety as long as the war lasted, should be to screen her from all harm, and that his fondest care through his whole life should be to protect her and make her happy.

Unusual circumstances and extraordinary excitement often cause the customary rules and practices of life to be abandoned; and so it was now. Marie received the love that was offered her, frankly, affectionately, and with her whole heart. She owned to her lover how well and truly she had loved him, and there, before her brother and his wife, plighted to him her troth, and promised to him then the obedience and love, which she soon hoped to owe him as his wife. Such declarations are usually made in private, but the friends now assembled had no secrets from each other, and they all felt that strange times made strange scenes necessary.

They then arranged their plans for the morrow. The day had already been an eventful one, but they little dreamed how much more was to be done before the morrow's sun was in the heavens; and yet even then they did not separate for the night: luckily for them all, they determined that too much was to be done to allow them yet to retire to rest.

It was resolved that on the following day they should leave Clisson for Durbellière, and hand over the château and all it contained—the farm and all its well-filled granaries, the cattle and agricultural wealth of the estate, to the fire and plunder of the republicans. The plate, however, they thought they could save, as well as the ladies' jewels and clothes, and other precious things which might be quickly packed and easily moved. They went to work at once to fill their trunks and baskets; and as the means of conveyance were then slow, de Lescure went out into the stables, and had the waggon prepared at once, and ordered that the oxen which were to draw it should be ready to start at three o'clock, in order that the load, if possible, might reach Durbellière the same night.

Master and mistress, servants and guests, worked hard, and at about two o'clock, the hour at which Westerman and his troop were starting for their quick ride, they had completed their task.

"You have killed yourself, dearest love," said Henri, pressing his arm round Marie's waist.

"Oh, no!" said she, smiling, but still so weary that she could hardly have stood unless he had held her; "I have not fought and conquered ten thousand republicans; but I don't know how you must feel."

Henri, however, insisted that she should go to bed and she, delighted to show her first act of obedience to his will, did as he desired her. She was soon undressed; she offered her prayers to heaven for her brother and sister-in-law, but with a stronger fervour for the dear companion and protector to whom she had sworn to devote her life, and then she laid her head upon her pillow, intending to think over her happiness; a few moments, however, were sufficient to change her half fearful thoughts of love and danger into blessed dreams of love and happiness. Poor girl! she did not long enjoy her happy rest.

De Lescure and Henri determined to remain up till the departure of the waggon. Madame de Lescure went up to her room, and the two gentlemen went down towards the farmyard. The waggon stood at the kitchen-door already packed, and the two servants were bringing the oxen down the road to yoke them to it.

"Go out at the front gate, François, and by the church at Terves; it is the better road. You will remain a couple of hours in Bressuire. We shall overtake you before you reach Beaulieu."

The servant acknowledged his master's commands, and fastened the last rope which bound the oxen to their burden. He spoke to his beasts, and accompanied his word with a goad from a pointed stick he held in his hand, when his farther progress was stopped by Henri's calling from a little distance down the road.

"Stop, François, stop!" said he. "Charles, come here; some one is coming hither at the top of his speed. Don't you hear the noise of hoofs upon the road?"

De Lescure ran to him, and kneeling down, put his ear to the ground. "It's a donkey or a mule," said he; "it is not a horse's foot."

"Come down the avenue," said Henri, "and let us see who it is. Whether mule or horse, the beast is going at his full speed."

"Better stay where we are," said de Lescure. "If he be coming to us, his news will reach the house quicker than by our going to meet him."

The rider grew nearer and nearer, and in a few moments turned up the road leading to the back of the house. The steps of the tired brute became slower as he trotted up the avenue, although the sound of a cudgel on his ribs were plainly audible. Henri and de Lescure were standing under the garden wall, and as the animal drew near them, they saw it was a jaded donkey, ridden by a peasant girl.

"Fly, for the sake of God!" said the girl, even before she dismounted from the donkey; "fly for the sake of the blessed Virgin. Take the ladies from the château, or they will be burnt—be burnt—be burnt!"

As she screamed the last words she slipped from the donkey, and almost fainted with the exertion she had undergone. She was the daughter of one of M. de Lescure's servants, and had been sent from Clisson into service at the château, from whence Westerman started on his expedition. When the republicans made their appearance there, she had fled with the other servants, but she had hung about the house, and about an hour and a half before Westerman left the place she learnt, through some of the soldiers, his intention of attacking Clisson that night.

"Who is coming to burn us, Marian?" said de Lescure, endeavouring by his own assumed coolness to enable her to collect her thoughts and power of speech.

"The blues—the blues!" screamed the girl. "They had all but overtaken me when I got to the short cut through the wood. There they are, there they are," and the noise of the advancing troop was distinctly audible through the stillness of the night.

The poor girl was quite exhausted, and fell to the ground fainting. De Lescure and Henri had both stood still for a moment, after having been made to comprehend that an immediate attack was about to be made on the château, but it was only for a moment.

"We must carry them through the wood, Charles," said Henri, whispering. "It is our only chance."

"True—true," said de Lescure. "Turn the oxen, Francois, turn them back through the yard into the farm-road, and then keep to the left into the wood. We will meet you at the seven limes."

"Take Victorine out through the garden," said Henri to his cousin, who was now hurrying into the house, "and through the iron gate. I saw the other day that the key was in it, and we can turn it. I tried it myself. I will bring Marie after you."

Henri stayed a moment to assist in turning the cumbrous waggon, and ran back to open the farm gates.

"Close the gates after you, Francois," said he, "and put the tressels close against them. If you lose a minute in doing it, you will gain five in delaying these devils. If you hear them following you in the wood-road, draw the waggon across the track and leave it."

He was only delayed two minutes by going back to the yard gates, but those two minutes were nearly fatal to him and Marie. Marian also delayed him again as he returned to the house.

"Where am I to go, M. Henri," said she; "what am I to do? they will be sure to kill me, for they saw me at Amaillou, and will know that I gave the warning."

"Hide yourself, my girl," said Henri: "hide yourself, but not in the house, for that will soon be a mass of ruins. Hide yourself in the woods; there cannot be many of these devils here, and they will not remain long."

He hurried into the house as he ceased speaking, and at the moment he did so Westerman and his thirty men turned the corner of the avenue. He rushed from the back door through the passages of the château into the hall, where he seized hold of a large cloak belonging to de Lescure, which he threw over his shoulder as he ran up stairs. On the stairs he met his cousin, with Madame de Lescure and the nurse and child.

"Haste, Henri, for God's sake, haste," said she; "I heard the tramp of their horses through my open window."

De Lescure had opened the summer door leading into the garden as he came up stairs, to have it ready for his exit, and he, and those under his care, escaped through it into the garden.

"Shut the garden door," roared Henri to him from the top of the staircase. "Shut the door, whatever you do." De Lescure could not understand his object, but he trusted his cousin, and closed the door as he passed through it. Henri had perceived that it would be impossible for him to regain the hall, and had resolved to jump from the window of the staircase into the garden, with his precious burden in his arms. He foresaw that if the door were left open, pursuit through it would be both inevitable and fatal.

Marie's room was close to the top of the stairs, and her lover did not use much ceremony in opening the door. In going to and from his wife's chamber, de Lescure had not passed it, and therefore the innocent girl slept soundly till Henri's sudden entrance roused her from her dreams.

"Who's that—who's that," said she, raising her head upon her pillow. The window curtains of the room were hardly closed, and she recognised immediately Henri's tall figure, and singular costume. "Oh! Henri, what has happened? what brings you here?"

"Rise, dearest, we must fly," said he: "we have not a moment—we fear the blues are coming." He dreaded that she would have lost all power of motion, had he told her that they were already beneath the windows.

"Haven't I time to dress?" said she; "I won't be a moment—not one minute."

"No, darling," answered he, raising her from the bed, as though she were an infant, and folding her in her brother's cloak. "We haven't one instant to throw away. Remember who has you in his arms: remember that it is I, your own Henri, who am pressing you to my heart." He took her up from the bed in his left arm, and with his right hand arraigned the cloak around her person, and carrying her out into the passage, hurried to the window which he had left open.

This window looked from the opposite end of the house to that at which Westerman found the open door. It was on the first landing of the staircase, and was therefore distant from the ground but little more than half the height of the ground floor, but a hard gravel path ran immediately under it; and though the leap was one which few young men might much hesitate to take with empty arms, it was perilous with such a burden as Henri had to carry. He however did not think twice about it, and would have considered himself and his charge nearly safe could he have reached the window unmolested, but that he was not allowed to do.

As he began to descend the stairs the loud noise of the troopers' boots, and the quick voice of Westerman giving his commands in the hall, told him at once that the house was already occupied by the blues. Even then, at that awful moment, he rejoiced at his precaution in having desired de Lescure to close the garden door. He took a large horse pistol from his belt, and holding it by the barrel, jumped down three stairs at a time, and already had his foot on the sill of the open window, when serjeant Craucher, who had been the first of the blues to enter the house, rushing up the stairs, succeeded in getting hold of the cloak which covered Marie. He pulled it from off her neck and shoulders, and her beautiful dark clustering curls fell down over Henri's shoulder. Her pale face, and white neck and bosom were exposed: her eyes were fast closed, as though she expected instant death, but both her arms were tightly fastened round her lover.

Craucher stumbled in his hurry in rushing up the stairs, but he still held fast to the collar of the cloak.

"I must stop your further journey, my pretty dear," said he: "the night air is not good for you—by heavens it's the red—"

He never finished his speech, or attempted to make another. On entering the back door he had struck his brazen head-piece against the lintel; the shock had broken the clasp, and his head was consequently bare. As he pulled at the cloak, Henri raised his right arm powerfully, and drove the butt-end of the pistol which he held, right through his skull, and scattered his brains upon the staircase. The grasp of the dying man was so firm that he could not extricate the cloak from his fingers. He saw that his only chance of escape was to relinquish it; he did so, and as he leapt from the window to the ground, poor Marie had nothing round her but her slight night dress.

Henri stumbled as he came to the hard gravel, but still he allowed no portion of Marie's body to touch the ground. He recovered himself in a moment, and made for the iron gate leading from the garden to the wood, through which de Lescure and his wife had escaped.

As Henri leapt from the window Westerman's eye had caught sight of the red scarf, and he knew that it was Larochejaquelin who was escaping. He rushed himself to the window, though, had he known it, he might have gone into the garden through the door, which was close at his hand. He leapt on the path, and was immediately on Henri's track. It was about three hundred yards from the house to the iron gate, and when Westerman was again on his feet, Henri had covered two thirds of the distance.

Run now, Henri, run your best, for the load you carry is heavy, and the German is strong and light of foot; his pistols, too, are loaded, and he well knows how to use them; but yours are empty, and you will not find another bare skull opposed to your heavy right hand; run, dear friend, and loving cousin; run faster with that precious trembling burden of yours, or all you have yet done, will have been done in vain.

But what avails his running: he did run fast and well, laden as he was, and fatigued with no ordinary day's work: he gained the gate, while as yet his pursuer was above a hundred yards behind him; but of what avail would that be, if he were obliged to leave the passage free for his enemy: it was impossible that he should continue to hold his ground, while he carried the fainting girl in his arms. It was then that that wonderful presence of mind, in the midst of the most urgent danger, of which Henri Larochejaquelin showed so many instances during war, stood him in stead, and saved two lives, when salvation seemed impossible.

In wandering about the place some days before, he had passed through this gate, and observing that the key stood in the lock, he had idly turned it backwards and forwards, locking and relocking the gate without an object; he had then observed that though the key worked easily, there was something wrong about the wards which prevented him from drawing it out after the lock was turned. The gate was made of iron bars, which were far enough asunder to allow of his hand and arm being passed through, so that when outside the gate he could then turn the key which was on the inside.

All these particulars he remembered in that moment of agony, and resolved what he would do to overcome the difficulties which they threw in his way. Having passed through the gate, he dropped his now senseless companion beneath the shelter of the wall, and passing his hands through the bars, turned the key and locked it. He then took out a short hunting-knife which he wore, and passing that also through the bars of the gate, he inserted it in the handle of the key, and then wrenching it round with all his force, broke the key in the wards: all the smiths in Poitou could not have locked the gate closer, or made it more impossible to open it.

Though the feat is tedious to explain, it did not take half a minute in performance; but still it allowed Westerman to come within pistol shot of him before he could get beneath the shelter of the wall. The German, however, in his anxiety to get through the gate, omitted to fire, though he had the pistol in his hand; he seized hold of the iron bars and shook them impotently: strong as he was, the gate was much too firm to be moved by his strength; the wall was twelve feet high, and utterly beyond his power to scale without a ladder.

He felt that he was foiled, and returned to the château to wreak his vengeance upon the inhabitants who might be left there, and on the furniture and walls of the house itself.

Henri pursued his way unopposed, and at the appointed spot, a little greensward surrounded by seven lime trees, he found his cousin and the rest of the party waiting for him, as well as François with the waggon.

"Is she safe—is she alive?" asked Madame de Lescure, almost frantic with grief and fear.

"She is alive, and I believe unhurt," said Henri; "but I fear she is senseless. She is quite undressed, too, as I was obliged to leave the cloak in which I had covered her, in the dying grasp of a trooper whom I killed." He gently laid her down, with her head in the lap of her kind sister, and then turned his back upon the party, that he might not gaze on the fair bosom, which was all exposed, and the naked limbs, which her dishevelled night dress did not suffice to cover.

Madame de Lescure and her nurse hastened to strip themselves of a portion of their clothes; it had been lucky that neither of them were undressed at the time of the attack, and though they were ill-prepared for a long journey, having neither caps nor strong shoes, nor shawls of any kind, yet they contrived between them to dress poor Marie decently. The nurse gave her shoes and stockings, declaring that going barefoot would not trouble her the least, and before many minutes had been wasted, they were again ready to proceed.

De Lescure and Henri had not lost these precious moments: the waggon was again put into motion: the three men carefully armed themselves: they loaded their pistols, for among the goods they were taking away, was the little remnant of gunpowder which was left among them: they decided that on hearing the first sound of pursuit, they would leave the waggon, and betake themselves to the thickest part of the woods; but both de Lescure and Henri were of opinion that they would not be followed.

"There cannot be many of them," said Henri, "and what there are, are all mounted. They are the German hussars; I know them by their brazen helmets. They won't attempt to follow us through the woods."

"They would have been after us before now had they intended doing so," said de Lescure. "The way was clear for them through the farm-yard, François, was it not?"

"No, Monseigneur," said François. "It was anything but clear. I turned the big bull out of his stall into the yard as I came out, and closed the gate behind me: he would gore a dozen of them before they could make their way through."

Whether the pursuit was arrested by the bull, or prevented by any other cause, the fugitives were not interrupted. They walked wearily and painfully, but yet patiently, and without a complaint above a league, before the women ventured to get upon the waggon. They then got out upon the road to Bressuire, at no great distance from that town, and on reaching Bressuire they got refreshment and proper clothes, and hired a voiture for the remainder of their journey.

Marie had hardly spoken from the moment when Henri dragged her from her bed, to that in which he helped her in the waggon; but after she had been sitting for a while, she indulged in a flood of tears, which she had restrained as long as she felt that her life depended on her exertions, and then calling Henri to her side, she thanked him, as she so well knew how to do, for all he had done for her.

"You have saved my life, dearest, now," said she, "and ten times more than my life; but I will not say that I love you better than I did before. Had I not known that it was your arms which were around me, I must have died when that horrid countenance glared over me on the stairs. Have I dreamt since, or was I really looking upon that face, when the agony of death came across it?" And as she asked the question, she closed her eyes, and her whole body trembled violently.

"I will tell you all that happened another time, love," said he; "we will not talk of these things now. A day or two at Durbellière will restore you to your spirits, and then we will rejoice over our escape."

They got into a voiture at Bressuire, and from thence continued their journey in something more like comfort, while Francois with the waggon followed them; but the two ladies were not destined to reach Durbellière that night. When they were about half-way between Bressuire and the château, they were met by a man on horseback, who was already on his way to Clisson. It was Jean Stein, who was hurrying as fast as his beast could carry him from Durbellière to M. Larochejaquelin; but instead of explaining now what was the purport of his errand, we will return to Clisson, and see how Westerman finished there the task he had undertaken.

When he found himself foiled at the gate, he returned as quickly as possible to the house. His men had already ransacked every room, and in their anxiety to find the more distinguished inhabitants of the château, allowed the domestics to escape; but few of them had been in bed, and even they were overlooked in the anxiety of the troopers to find M. de Lescure. They did not dream that any warning could have been given to the château, nor could they conceive it possible that at three o'clock in the morning the royalists should have been up, and ready for instant flight. It was not till nearly five that they satisfied themselves that neither de Lescure nor his wife, nor any of his family were in the house; and then, at the command of their General, they commenced the work of destruction.

The troopers got hay and straw from the farm-yard (not without some opposition from the loose bull,) and piled them in every room in the château; they then took the furniture, beds, curtains, wearing apparel, and every article of value they could find, and placed them in heaps, in such a way as to render them an immediate prey to the flames. They did the same to the barns and granaries, in which there were large stores of corn, and also to the stables, in which stood the horses and cattle; the bull, which François had loosened, was the only animal about the place that did not perish. Having systematically prepared the château and out-houses for a huge bonfire, they put a light to the straw in various places, and re-mounting their horses, stood around it till they saw that no efforts which the peasants might use could extinguish the flames. Westerman then gave the word of command for their return; they started at a sharp trot, and he did not allow them to slacken their pace till he had again passed the ruins of the little village of Amaillou.

While the troopers were thus preparing to set the château in a blaze, the General himself was not idle; he seated himself in the salon, and having had pen, ink, and paper brought to him, he wrote the following despatch to the President of the Convention, in which, it will be observed, he studiously omitted all mention of the defeat which he had incurred between Amaillou and Clisson, and the retreat which his army had been forced to make. The date is given in the denomination which will be intelligible to the reader, as the Fructidors and the Messidors, Brumaires and Nivoses, which had then been adopted by the republicans, now convey no very defined idea to people, who have not yet scrupled to call the months by their old aristocratic names, or to count the year from their Saviour's birth.

"Château of Clisson, July 1798.

"Citizen President,

"I have the honour to acquaint you that I have already succeeded in carrying the arms of the Convention as far as the residence of the most powerful of the rebel leaders. As I am writing, my men are preparing to set fire to this den of aristocratic infamy, and within an hour the stronghold of the redoubted de Lescure will be level with the ground.

"This wretched country is so crowded with ravines and rocks, and the roads are so narrow, so deep, and so bad, that I have been forced to make my way hither with a small detachment of thirty men only, but I have found that sufficient to drive the tiger from his lair. He, and the other rebel leader, Larochejaquelin, have fled into the woods, without either money, arms, or even clothing; and I doubt not soon to be able to inform the Convention that, at any rate, they can never again put themselves at the head of a rebellious army.

"Citizen President, deign to receive from my hands the only trophies which I have deemed myself justified in rescuing from the flames which are about to consume this accursed château. I enclose the will and a miniature portrait of the aristocrat, de Lescure.

"I pray you to receive, and to make acceptable to the Convention, the most distinguished,

"&c. &c. &c.

"WESTERMAN"

CHAPTER IX
SANTERRE

Santerre and Adolphe Denot left the main army at Thouars, and made their way to Argenton with about four thousand men. From thence, Durbellière was distant about four leagues; and Santerre lost no time in making his preparations for destroying that château, as Westerman was at the same moment doing at Clisson. Generally speaking, the people of the towns, even in La Vendée sided with the republicans; but the people of Argenton were supposed to be royalists, and Santerre therefore gave positive orders that every house in it should be destroyed. He did not, however, himself want to see the horrid work done, but hurried on to Durbellière, that he might, if possible, surprise the Vendean chiefs, whom he believed to be staying there. About one hundred and fifty men followed him, and the remainder of the army was to march on to Bressuire, as soon as Argenton was in ashes.

Santerre, since he had left the company of the other Generals at Thouars, had become more familiar and confidential with Denot, and rode side by side with him from Argenton, talking freely about the manners of the country, and the hopes of the royalists, till he succeeded in getting the traitor into good humour, and obtaining from him something like a correct idea of the state of the country.

"And this is the parish of St. Aubin?" said Santerre, as they drew near to Durbellière.

"Yes," said Denot, "this is the parish of St. Aubin; and the estate of the Larochejaquelins."

"And they are popular with the people?" said Santerre. "They must have been well loved, or they would not have been so truly followed."

Denot blushed at the heavy accusation against himself which these words conveyed; but he made no answer.

"And this old man, my friend?" said Santerre, "this ancient cripple that you tell me of? he is too old, too infirm, I suppose, to care much about this revolt?"

"Not at all," said Denot; "no one in the country is more anxious for success than the old Marquis."

"There you are again, friend," said Santerre, "I know you'll get your neck into danger. Have I not told you that the Republic knows nothing of Marquises?"

"I only called him by the name he goes by, as you'd call a man Peter, if his name were Peter. I didn't mean to say he was a Marquis," said Denot, excusing himself.

"But you mustn't say so at all, unless you speak of him as a criminal, as you would speak of a perjurer, or a parricide. But as to this foolish old man; is he not doting? If I thought that, I might perhaps be excused in sparing him."

"Doting!" said Denot; "not at all; he has all his faculties as much as you or I."

Santerre gave a look of disgust at the wretch, who would not even follow his hint by giving such an account as might spare the life of the old man, who had been his host, his guardian, and his friend. He said nothing further, however, but trotted on quickly, till the cherry groves of Durbellière were in sight, and then he halted to give his final orders to his men, and make arrangements that the house should be surrounded.

"You remember our bargain, citizen General?" said Denot.

"What bargain?" asked the brewer.

"Why, about the young lady; the girl, you know," replied the other. "No one is to interfere between me and Agatha Larochejaquelin. She is to be my prize and my reward."

"I will be as good as my word," said Santerre, "as long as you are true to yours; but I own I pity the young lady the treatment she is likely to receive from her lover," and as he spoke, he rode up to the front door of the house, accompanied by Denot and a company of men on horseback.

The immediate arrival of republican soldiers in the neighbourhood of Durbellière was neither expected, or even feared by the inhabitants of the château, or it would not have been left by Henri, as it had been, perfectly undefended. The truth was this: the royalists had hitherto been so very generally successful against the republicans; and that, when every odds of number, arms, and position had been in favour of their enemies, that they had learnt to look with contempt upon the blues, as they called them. Hitherto the royalists had always been the attacking party; the republicans had contented themselves with endeavouring to keep their position within the towns; and when driven from thence, had retreated altogether out of the revolted district. Except lately at Nantes, the Vendeans had as yet incurred no great reverse; they had not, therefore, learnt to fear that their houses would be attacked and burnt; their corn and cattle destroyed; and even their wives and children massacred. The troops which had now been dispatched by the Convention for the subjection of the country, were of a very different character from those with whom the Vendeans had as yet contended, and the royalists were not long before they experienced all the horrors of a civil war, in which quarter was refused them by their enemies, and mercy even to children was considered as a crime.

When Santerre rode up to the door of the château, ten men might have taken possession of Durbellière. It was a fine July evening, about seven o'clock. The old Marquis had been wheeled in his easy chair out of the house, to the top of the broad steps which led from the back of the château into the garden. Agatha was sitting at his feet on the top step, reading to him, and the little Chevalier Mondyon, who retained no semblance of the soldier about his person, except the red scarf round his waist, was seated straddle-legged atop of one of the huge white lions which guarded the entrance.

"Agatha, I hear horsemen," said the boy, jumping off his seat. "There—there—quite plain!"

"It is Henri and Charles coming from Clisson," said Agatha.

"If it be, they have a troop of cavalry with them," said the Chevalier. "Perhaps it's the Prince de Talmont, for I think they have not so many horsemen with them in the south," and the little Chevalier ran out to greet, as he thought, his gallant friends.

"Whoever they be, Agatha," said the old Marquis, "give them a warm welcome if they come in the King's name. They will know that I cannot rise to meet them, but make them welcome to everything in and about the château."

Agatha had closed her book, and was rising to execute her father's wishes, when Momont, the grey-haired butler, hurrying round from the kitchen-door as fast his old legs would carry him, screamed out: "The blues! the blues!"

Agatha, who was in the act of entering the house as she heard the fearful cry, turned instantly back to her father's side. She was deadly pale, but she spoke not a word. She grasped her father's hand, and fixed herself close to his chair, determined in that position to await the worst that her enemies could do her.

"Run, Agatha, run," said the Marquis, "into the garden, my dear love. The gate will be open at the back. Run, Agatha, for your life!" Agatha, however, did not stir.

"Do you hear me, Agatha?" continued the old man, wildly supplicating her to go from him. "Do you hear me, my daughter? If you would have my blessing before I die, do as I bid you now. What are my grey hairs to your young life, that you should sacrifice yourself for me?"

It was of no avail, for the daughter stood fast by her disabled father's side, grasping his right hand so that nothing should tear her from him, and turning her beautiful face towards the house, watching for the approach of her enemies. Nor had she to watch long; before the Chevalier had been gone five minutes, Santerre, with his sword drawn, tramped heavily through the house, followed by Denot, and a score of his men. The door from the salon to the garden steps was open, and without waiting a moment in the house, he marched through and confronted Agatha and her father.

"Here is your damsel safe, at any rate, friend Denot," said Santerre, "and a pretty girl she is too, but a bitter royalist, no doubt, by the proud turn of her white neck."

Denot did not immediately follow Santerre on to the steps. He had firmly resolved to thrust himself upon Agatha as a conqueror; to rush upon her as an eagle upon its prey, and to carry her off with a strong hand, disregarding her cries, as the eagle disregards the bleating of the lamb; but the first glance he had got of his victim somehow startled his resolve, and scared the blood from his cheek, and almost from his heart. When Santerre, however, called to him, he was obliged to follow; and then, making fearful grimaces with his lips, and scowling with his eyes, he stalked out before the astonished father and daughter.

"Yes, Agatha," he said, looking full upon her, but not daring to turn an eye upon the countenance of her much more indignant father, "yes, Agatha, I have come, as I told you I would come—I have come to claim you, and no power shall now gainsay me. I have come to seize you as my own; to take you with a strong hand, and an out-stretched arm. My prayers were of no avail; you shall find that my sword is more powerful. When last I sought you, it was as a suppliant, I now come for you as a conqueror. Come, Agatha, you are now mine. All the powers of earth shall not rescue you from my arms."

"You appear to me, Sir, to come as a traitor," said Agatha.

"A good republican, my dear," said Santerre: "he comes as a good republican."

Agatha did not deign to make any further reply, but as Santerre and the men had now left the steps and gone into the house, Denot put his hand on her arm to lead her away from her father's side.

"Leave her alone," shouted the old man, now speaking for the first time since his eyes had rested on the republican soldiers. "Leave her alone, thou false wretch, thou basest of all miscreants. Touch her not, or—or—," and the poor Marquis strove in vain to rise from his chair to his daughter's help. "Momont, Chapeau, Arthur—Arthur," he halloed. "My daughter—my daughter, oh! my daughter!"

No one, however, came to his aid, and Agatha, finding resistance to be in vain, suffered Denot to lead her into the house, without uttering another word.

Not the slightest resistance was made to Santerre and his men; he took possession of the château without a word even being said to stop him. The servant girls hid themselves in the garrets, but were soon brought down again, and bade to set quiet in the hall, till their fate should have been decided on. Momont attempted to conceal himself in the garden, but he was soon found and brought back again, and stationed among the women. Chapeau was not seen at all, and even the little Chevalier was missing for a time, though he returned of his own accord before Santerre had been long in possession of the place.

Santerre seated himself with two of his officers in the largest of the salons, and ordered that the old Marquis should be brought before him. He was rather perplexed as to what he should next do; his orders were to destroy everything—houses, property, and life; to spare neither age, sex, nor imbecility; and Santerre, undertaking the commission, had thought, in his republican zeal, that he would find no weakness in himself to militate against the execution of such orders. He was mistaken in himself, however. He had led the fierce mobs of Paris to acts of bloodshed and violence, but in doing so he had only assisted with an eager hand in the overthrow of those who he thought were tyrannizing over the people. He had stood by at the execution of a King, and ordered the drums to beat to drown the last words of the dying monarch; but the King had been condemned by those whom Santerre looked on as the wisest and best of the nation; and in acting as he had done, he had been carried on as well by ideas of duty as excitement. He found his present a much more difficult task. Indeed, after sitting still for some few minutes in that easy chair, meditating what he would do next, he found that the work which he had undertaken was one which he literally could not go through with.

"Is the old gentleman there?" said he; and as he asked, the Marquis, with his eyes closed, and his hands crossed on his breast, was wheeled into the room. Agatha was seated, or rather was crouching, on a sofa in the corner, for Adolphe Denot was standing over her uttering threats and words of love alternately, the latter of which, however, sounded by far the most horrible in poor Agatha's ears.

"Give me a pen and paper," said Santerre, and having got them, he continued writing for a minute or two. "Now, my old friend," said he, addressing the Marquis, "I am given to understand that you yourself, personally, have never lent a hand to this iniquitous revolt. Is it so?"

"I am too old and too infirm to carry a sword," said the Marquis, "but what little I could do for my King, I—."

"Exactly—exactly," said Santerre, interrupting him, "you are a cripple I see. There is no evidence wanting to show that you haven't taken up arms. It is this pestilent son of yours has brought you into trouble."

"He would have been no son of mine had he not acted as he has done," said the old man indignantly.

"Will you hold your silly tongue, my friend," said Santerre. "He is doting, quite doting, I see," and he turned round to his brother officers, as though appealing to them to corroborate his opinion.

"Either that, or else he must be very fond of Mademoiselle Guillotine," said one of them.

"Well, now, old gentleman, answer me this question," said Santerre, "do you want to die this evening?"

"If I could but think that my daughter was safe, and out of the power of that viper, whom I have warmed in my bosom, death would not be unwelcome to me."

"Viper!" said Denot, curling his lips, and speaking through his closed teeth. "Warmed in your bosom! I have yet to learn, old man, that I owe you ought; but if it be a comfort to you to know it, know that no worse evil awaits your daughter than to become the wife of a true Frenchman."

"True!" said the Marquis. "Yes, as true as the Prince of Darkness."

"Come, old man," said Santerre, "we know nothing about Princes, nor yet about Marquises. You must be content now to call the devil by his plain name, though I rather believe it has already been decided in Paris, that the gentleman is nothing but a foul fiction of the aristocrats. Come, if you wish to save your neck, put your signature to this little document."

"I will sign nothing that is put before me in such a manner," said the Marquis.

"Why you have not even read it. Take the pen in your hand, I tell you; it is only a proclamation of the truth, that you have not taken up arms against the republic."

Agatha understood the object of the republican General, though her father did not. She sprang from the corner in which Denot had placed her, and coming close to her father, whispered to him.

"The gentleman means well to you, father, though his words are rough. He wishes to save us. He will save both of us, father, if he can. Read the paper, and if there be nothing absolutely untrue in it, put your name to it."

"Read it yourself, Agatha," said he, "and if you then tell me to sign it, I will do so."

Agatha took up the paper which Santerre had written, and read, but not aloud, the following words:

"I hereby proclaim myself a true son of the Republic, and a citizen brother of all free Frenchmen. I declare that I have never carried arms against the Convention myself, and demand that I may not be accounted responsible for any misguided members of my family, who may have done so."

Twice Agatha read the words, and as she did so, her father's eyes rested anxiously on her face. "Well, my child," said he, "your father's honour is in your hands; tell me what I am to do," and he mechanically held the pen within his fingers, which Santerre had thrust into his hand.

"We will die, father," said she, "if these men please it," and she put down the document on the table on which it had been written. "I cannot ask you to denounce our dear, our gallant Henri. I cannot bid you to deny your King. Death at any rate will not dishonour us. We will only beg of this gentleman that in his mercy he will not separate us," and putting her arm round her father's neck, she fastened her hand upon the folds of his coat, as though determined that nothing should again separate her from his side.

"Denounce Henri!" said the old man; "denounce my own dear, gallant son, the most loyal of those who love their King—the bravest of the brave! No, Sir! I give you no thanks for your mercy, if you intended any. I, and my daughter, Sir, cannot bear arms for our King; she by reason of her sex, and I from my infirmities; but, Sir, we can die for him; we can die for him as readily as the bravest who falls in the first ranks of the battle. Had I still so much power in my own house as to command a cup of wine, I would drink my last pledge to my royal master—but it matters not; the heart and the will are still the same," and taking off the tasselled velvet cap which he wore, he waved it above his head, exclaiming, "Vive le Roi! vive le Roi!"

"The accursed, pestilent old fanatic!" said Santerre, spurning the table as he rose in his passion, and upsetting it into the middle of the room; and then he walked up and down the salon with rapid strides, trying to induce himself to give orders for the immediate execution of the staunch old royalist.

"What is to be done next, General?" said one of his officers, who did not quite admire the evident clemency of the brewer.

"The accursed, pestilent old fanatic!" he repeated between his teeth; and then he said, after drawing a long breath: "they must go to Paris, and let Fouquier Tinville deal with them. There may be secrets that I know not of. I think it better that they should go to Paris." And he felt relieved of a heavy load in having devised a scheme by which he could avoid having himself to give the order for the execution. "Let him be locked up, and well treated, mind you. He shall go to Saumur in his own carriage, and Barrère may send him to Paris how he pleases, or to the devil if he chooses."

"And the servants, General?"

"Oh! ah, yes, the servants!" said Santerre, walking out into the hall to inspect them; "women, an't they? What, five, six, seven, nine women, one old man, and a boy; well, I suppose we must have them out in a row, and shoot them."

Down on their knees went the nine women and the boy, imploring that their innocent lives might be spared to them. Momont, like his master, had still some spirit in his bosom, and kept his seat, saying to himself, but out loud, "I told him so—I told him so. I told him that we who remained here needed as much courage as those who went to the wars; but now, he that talked so much, he's the only one to run away." The poor butler alluded to Chapeau, who had certainly been in the house a few minutes before the arrival of the republicans, and who as certainly had not been seen since.

"I suppose we must have them out before the house, and fire upon them?"

And he turned to the officer who was next to him, as though asking his advice.

"If you ask my advice, General, I would make no difference between the lot; ten minutes should see the last of the whole set of them—the old man, his daughter, and the rest. If we are to send every master of a family with his children up to Paris, or even to Saumur, the tribunals can never do their work, nor can the guillotines fall half fast enough for them."

"When I ask your advice on one subject, Captain, I do not expect you to give it me on another," said Santerre. "Sergeant, take those women out, and the old man, and the boy, stand them in a line upon the gravel plot there, and bring a file of musketeers." And the republican General again began pacing up and down the room, as though he did not at all like the position in which his patriotic zeal had placed him.

The poor women were dragged by their limbs out before the door, screeching as they went, and filling the air with their loud, agonizing cries. Momont walked after them, with his head hanging down, his knees shaking, and his back bent double; but still he was walking himself; he was still able to save himself the disgrace of being dragged out like the women. When he got to the front door, he attempted to totter back, but a republican soldier stopped him.

"My master! my dear master!" said Momont, "let me but kiss his hand, and I will come back."

The soldier let him pass in, and the old man in a moment was at his master's feet. "God bless you, Monseigneur!" said he, "God bless you! Say one word of kindness to your servant, before he is shot for loving his master and his King."

The Marquis put his hand on the grey hairs of the old butler, and moved his lips, but he said nothing: the power of speech for the time failed him; the energy he had displayed, and the excitement he had felt, had been too much for him, and he was unable to reply aloud to the blessing of his faithful servant.

"God bless you, Momont," said Agatha, calmly, as she stood close to her father, still holding to his coat, and supporting his head against her body. "Let your last thoughts be of the Saviour who died for you, and so shall your death be only the end of all your troubles."

He was not allowed to remain longer on his knees, but was hurried back to the spot where the women were awaiting their doom. The soldiers could not get them to stand; they were crouching down on the ground in all positions, one or two with their heads almost buried in the earth, one or two kneeling, and still screaming for mercy. The old housekeeper had fallen on her haunches, and was looking up to heaven, while she wildly struck the ground with her hands; the poor page had made a last, but futile effort to escape with the aid of his heels, but he had been at once caught, and was now bound by his waist to a tree, which grew close to the road on which the wretched party were huddled; the poor boy had quite forgotten his attempt at manhood and mingled his loud screams with those of the women.

"General," said the sergeant, stepping up to him, "the men are ready; will you give the word to fire?"

Two salons, one looking to the front of the house, and the other to the back, communicated with each other by folding-doors, which were now wide open. Santerre, the Marquis, Denot, Agatha, and the other republican officer, were in the back room; the unfortunate wretches doomed to die were collected on the gravel before the windows of the front room; the carabineers who were to fire on them stood in a double file on the broad area before the front door, and above the steps. Santerre, on being addressed by the sergeant, stalked into the front room to give the order; his altered face plainly shewed the strong passion which was at work within his heart. As he passed from one room to the other, he threw his cap upon the ground, and trampled on it; then clenched his fist, and bit his lip till the blood ran. The fatal word "Fire" was on his tongue; but, without intending it, he looked through the window, and his eyes fell on the wretched creatures who were expecting death, and he was unable to give the command. He sank back upon a chair, and hiding his face in both his hands, he said to the sergeant, in a low voice:

"They must get some one else for this work, I am not the man I thought I was." He then rose and said, in a voice he vainly attempted should appear calm and dignified, "Sergeant, keep the prisoners in custody this night: I have changed my mind. Be ready to march at four tomorrow morning. We will have a bonfire to light us on our journey: see that there are plenty of faggots ready before you let the men sleep."

The poor women were unable to raise themselves and walk away, when they were made to understand that they were not to die that night. Some prayed, others screamed almost louder than before: one or two of them fainted, and continued fainting the greater part of the night: they were all of them taken into the house, and kept together in the kitchen surrounded by a guard.

"Citizen General!" said Denot to Santerre, stepping up to him after this scene was over; "I have performed my part of my engagement I believe."

"Well, man, supposing you have; what do you want? Are you going to grumble because I have not slaughtered the wretches you have betrayed to me?"

"Not at all, General; you know your own duty, doubtless. I am going to return to Saumur, to which place I desire an escort for myself and this young lady."

"By heaven I pity her!" said Santerre. "I don't know what has come to me tonight, that I should trouble myself with the cares of a swarm of aristocrats." And then he said, addressing Agatha, "Are you ready and willing, young woman, for a midnight ride with this hot young lover, who seems so fond of you?"

"She must be ready, General Santerre," said Denot, taking hold of Agatha's hand: "it is now my turn to command her: she must be ready, whether she be willing or no."

"You will not force me to leave my father?" said Agatha, appealing to Santerre. "You will not deliver a poor unprotected girl into the hands of such a maniac as that."

"Maniac!" said Denot. "But I care not; your words are to me like the empty wind: the time had gone by for words between you and me, when you refused to listen to those I addressed to you upon my knees. Come, Agatha, come; my heart's treasure—for still you are so; come, my love, my captive, and my bride!" And Denot essayed to go, as though he expected Agatha to follow him through the world like a tame dog.

"Oh, Sir, protect me from him!" said Agatha, still appealing to Santerre. "He is mad—you see and hear he is mad! I have not asked you for my life, nor do I so now; but I pray you, I beseech you, by the remembrance of the females who are dear to yourself save me from the power of that frantic man. Had he not been mad, had he not utterly lost his senses, he would have been the last to have brought you hither."

"I have thought something like that myself pretty one," said Santerre. "Come, Denot, you shall talk to the lady tomorrow; we will leave her with her father tonight." "Your word, General!" said Denot, assuming his furious look, "your plighted word and honour. Was she not to be my prize, my captive, my reward. You dare not go back from the promise you have made me."

"Nonsense, man alive," said Santerre. "You can't carry her off tonight. I believe in my heart she's right, and that you're as mad a man as ever roared in a hospital. Let go her arm, I tell you; you shall not drag her about in that way."

The Marquis, during this scene, was endeavouring to throw his arms round his daughter, so as to protect her; but his efforts were but of little avail. Agatha herself still held to her father by one hand, but the other she was unable to extricate from her persecutor's grasp. She did not scream or cry, for there was something within her—a memory of Cathelineau's last moments, of her brother's gallantry, and her father's loyalty, which strongly urged her to repress her tears before a republican; but her strength was almost gone, her nerves were all but over strung, when she heard a sudden noise behind her of some one rushing into the room, and Adolphe Denot quickly dropped her hand, and gave a yell of pain. He had received a sharp blow of a cherry switch across his face, and the blood was running from both his cheeks.

Santerre, and the other republican officers in the room, put their hands to their pistols, and prepared to defend themselves, but the only person who appeared was a young boy: to be sure he had the dreadful red scarf round his waist; but he had no weapon but his cherry stick, after having given Denot the blow across his face, he made no farther use of that. It was the little Chevalier who had arrived so opportunely; he took Agatha's hand in his, and pressed it closely, and took his place beside her without speaking a word.

"And who the deuce is this young bantam cock?" said Santerre.

"I am the little Chevalier Mondyon," said Arthur; "a true royalist, and sworn knight to Agatha Larochejaquelin. And that man there is a traitor and a false knave; he is not fit to be punished with a sword like a gentleman."

"Well crowed, my bantam," said Santerre; "and be good enough to tell me where you come from. No, friend Denot, no, we'll have no dagger work just at present." And putting his huge hand on the other's shoulder, he dragged him back as he was about to plunge his knife into the little Chevalier.

"I came from the cherry wood there," said Arthur. "Maybe you think I ought not to have run away, and deserted my lady love. Maybe I'm rather ashamed of my own self, but at any rate when you speak of it, say that I came back of my own accord. I'm not a bit afraid to die now," and as he spoke he squeezed Agatha's hand. His heart was full of apprehension, lest she should suspect for a moment that he had really fled from her through fear, but Agatha understood well his ready wit, and appreciated his more than boyish courage.

Santerre now made his arrangements for the night. All the inhabitants of the château were kept under strict surveillance. The Marquis, his daughter, and the Chevalier were allowed to remain together, and Denot was prevented from annoying them. At day-break the following morning Durbellière was to be burnt, and Santerre, with his prisoners, would then proceed to join Westerman at Bressuire.

"Let him slaughter them, if he likes," said he to himself, "I don't care what he says of me. I am at any rate too well known to be suspected. I don't know what came over me today, but had the Republic depended on it, I could not have done it," and he flung himself down on one of Agatha's sofas, and slept not the less soundly for having began his career of extermination in so vacillating a manner.

CHAPTER X
THE RESCUE

The little Chevalier had no intention of saving himself, and deserting his friends, when, on Santerre's approach, he ran off, leaving Agatha and the Marquis at the garden door of the château. He knew that Chapeau was at the smith's forge, with his own pony. He had himself sent him there; and as soon as he perceived, on running round the side of the house, that the whole front was occupied by the blues, his first idea was to go after his pony, and ride as fast as the animal could carry him to Echanbroignes, and bring the royalists from thence to the rescue of their friends at Durbellière. With this object he clambered over the garden-wall, and well knowing every foot of the ground, reached the forge in a few minutes. Chapeau and the smith were there, as was also the pony, and a breathless countryman was already telling them that the château was surrounded by the whole army of blues.

"Here's the Chevalier," said Chapeau, stopping the peasant in his story. "In the name of Heaven, M. Arthur, what is all this?"

"That traitor, Denot, has brought a parcel of blues down upon the château," said the Chevalier. "The Marquis and Mademoiselle Agatha are already in their hands; they will be murdered before morning. What is to be done? Oh! Chapeau, what are we to do to save them?"

"M. Denot!" said Chapeau. "You don't mean to say M. Denot has turned blue—"

"I saw him with my own eyes," said the boy; "he was one of the officers commanding the men; but there was another over him, a big, clumsy, noisy man; he it was I saw first of all, and Denot was behind him; and then there was a crowd of horsemen following them. Both drawing-rooms were full before we knew they were in the house at all."

"And how did you get through them, M. Arthur?" said Chapeau.

"I got over the wall behind the stables. I never went into the house at all. But what on earth are we to do, Chapeau? Can't we get the men from Echanbroignes to come to the rescue?"

The matter was then discussed between them, and it was decided that Chapeau should take the pony, and collect the men at Echanbroignes and on the road thither, and that he should return with them, if possible, during the night; that the smith should go off to St. Laud, and get Father Jerome to bring with him the men from thence, and that Arthur should return to the château.

"No," said he, when Chapeau pressed him to undertake the mission to Echanbroignes, "I will not leave Mademoiselle Agatha and the Marquis any longer. They will think I have run away. Besides, maybe, I can be of some service to them there. At any rate, I will go and see what is going on; but, Chapeau, our lives depend on you. Don't lose one single minute now, even though you should ride poor Bayard to death," and he put his hand on the neck of the pony, whom he had named after the flower of chivalry.

Chapeau and the smith started on their important missions, and the Chevalier slowly, but manfully, walked back to the château. No one stopped him as he walked through the open gates, and in at the back door. On getting into the hall, he heard the sound of the Marquis's voice, as he was praying Santerre to preserve his daughter from Denot, and then, hurrying into the room, he made use of the little cherry stick which he carried, in the manner which has been described.

None of the inhabitants of the château went to bed that night; indeed, the beds were all occupied by the troopers, who threw themselves down to sleep, without taking off their boots, wherever they could find any convenient place to lie down. To do Santerre justice, he repeatedly pressed the Marquis to go to his own room, assuring him that he should not be further disturbed than by the presence of a sentinel; but the old man insisted on remaining in the salon, and Agatha and the Chevalier sat with him. Santerre, and Denot, and a cavalry sergeant, remained in the same room, and a couple of sentinels were stationed on the top of the steps at the back of the house, and four at the front. None of the party in the salon slept, excepting Santerre; but they all sat silent; neither Arthur nor Agatha dared to speak to each other on the subject which at that time filled their thoughts. The night seemed dreadfully long to Arthur, and yet hardly long enough. He discovered soon after his return, that it was Santerre's purpose to burn the château early in the morning, and then to take the inhabitants away with him as prisoners; and he greatly feared that Chapeau would not be able to return in time to prevent the conflagration. He anxiously watched the first break of day, and listened intently, but for a long time in vain, for the noise of coming feet. About half-past two, a soldier came and whispered to the sergeant, who then woke Santerre, and whispered to him, but the General was sleepy, and did not wish his dreams should be disturbed. He muttered something to the sergeant, who again left him, and resumed the seat in which he had sat since he first entered the room. Denot had risen two or three times during the night, and paced rapidly and uneasily about. Whenever he had done so, Agatha had firmly grasped both her father's chair and the Chevalier's hand, as though she feared he was about to renew his attempts to drag her away, but he did not either touch her or speak to her. He was probably aware that the sergeant, who sat there without once closing his eyes through the long hours, had orders to prevent him from doing so.

The Chevalier had no watch, and could not see how the hours were going, but it seemed to him as though it were broad day. He thought it must be five, six, nay seven o'clock; and he could not understand why the lazy republicans remained so passive and so quiet, nor could he imagine why Chapeau was so long in coming. The whole affair seemed to him so strange that he could hardly help fancying that he was dreaming. There sat close to him his dear friend Agatha, with her eyes wide open, fixed on Denot, and she had been gazing in this way for hours after hours, without speaking a word. There was the Marquis close to her, equally silent, but also wide awake, though his eyes were closed. Arthur was sure that he was awake. There was Denot marching to and fro. Adolphe Denot, who but the other day was in the house, not only as a friend, but as a comrade, eager in the cause in which they were all embarked, as much at home in the château as Henri Larochejaquelin himself: and now he was the worst of traitors, and the most cruel of enemies—there was the sergeant of the republican army, sitting as quiet and composed as though he were merely idling his time away in his own barracks; and there was Santerre—the much talked of republican brewer and General; the sanguinary, remorseless, fanatic democrat; the sworn enemy of all that was noble, loyal and gentle, the dreaded Santerre; for the Chevalier had now learned the name of the big, clumsy, noisy man, whom he had seen leading his troops into the salon where he was now sleeping—there he was, sleeping fast: while care, anxiety, or a sense of duty banished sleep from all the others, he, who had so much more need than others to be watchful, was snoring loud, and dreaming of the denizens of the faubourgs, who used to love him so well. All this seemed to Arthur like a dream from which he could not awake—there were his enemies, his deadly enemies, before and around him. He knew that it was the practice of the republican soldiers to massacre all whom they took bearing arms against the Republic he had even heard that it was now their horrid purpose to go further than this, and to slaughter the inhabitants of the whole district which had revolted; at any rate his own doom would be death; he was certain that he had not many days, probably many hours, to live, unless Chapeau should arrive in time, and with sufficient force, to rescue the whole party. Yet he felt no fear; he could not sufficiently realize the position in which he found himself, to feel the full effects of its danger. The republican sergeant sat immediately in front of him, and each kept his eye fixed on the other's face; not that either of them had any object in doing so, any particular motive for watching the other's countenance, but soon after day-break the gaze of each had become fixed, and it seemed as though neither of them were able to turn away his eyes.

Arthur occupied his mind in speculating on the character of the soldier, in trying to guess from his features whether he were a cruel or a kind-hearted man; whether he were a ferocious democrat, eager for the blood of all who had been born in a rank above him, or merely a well-trained soldier, obeying the behests of those under whose orders it was his duty to act. The Chevalier had no idea that his own or his friends' fate depended in any way on the man's disposition; but such thoughts came across his brain unwittingly, and he could not restrain them. At last, he felt that he had a kind of intimacy with the sergeant; that if he should chance to meet him after three or four years had passed, he should greet him as an old acquaintance, whom he had well known, and he was sure that the sergeant had the same feeling respecting him.

The day dawned soon after two o'clock, and as by degrees the clear sun-light streamed in at the uncurtained windows, Arthur, in his impatience, thought that the day was advancing; but in reality it was not yet five o'clock, when Santerre, waking with a tremendous yawn, stretched his huge limbs, and then jumped up from the sofa on which he had been lying.

"Now for a bonfire," said he, "and then for breakfast; or perhaps we had better get our breakfast first, and have our bonfire afterwards. Old gentleman, I have no doubt my men took strange liberties with your cellar and larder last night. I hope they have left enough about the place to furnish you with the last meal you will ever eat in this château."

"I know, Sir, what soldiers are in a house," said the old man. "I will not say that your men are welcome here, for that would be falsehood; but I begrudge them nothing that they eat and drink."

"Well, that's kind of you; but, considering that all which is not now eaten and drunk, will be immediately wasted and spoilt, you would certainly be foolish to allow the consumption of your provisions to make you uneasy. Here, sergeant," and then Santerre spoke aside to the sergeant, and gave him various orders, which the man departed to obey.

"And now, General Santerre," said Denot, marching close up to him, "are you prepared to make good your promise to me? Are you prepared to give me an escort for myself and this lady, and to allow us to commence our journey from hence to Saumur?"

Denot's personal appearance had not been at all improved by the blow which Arthur had given him across his face. Both his cheeks were much swollen immediately beneath the eyes, and one of them was severely cut. He felt that his looks were against him, and he endeavoured to make up for the injury his countenance had sustained by the sternness of his voice, and the determined rigour of his eye. "I presume, General Santerre," added he, "that your plighted word is sufficient warrant to me for your good faith."

"There is the lady," said Santerre, pointing to Agatha. "I did not undertake to protect you from the wrath of any rivals you might have in her affections. It seems to me that at present she prefers that young dare-devil slip of aristocracy to your patriotic ardour. If she won't go to Saumur with you, I can't make her."

"By all the powers of heaven and hell, she shall go with me!" said Denot, advancing towards her.

"Beware the switch—beware the switch again, thou false knave!" said the little Chevalier, jumping up, and standing immediately before Agatha, with his cherry stick in his hand. Denot had no other arms about him but his dagger, and that he drew, as he advanced towards the boy.

"No daggers—I will have no daggers," shouted Santerre. "Sergeant, take the dagger from him, unless he puts it up."

"Beware the switch, thou traitor! beware the switch, thou knave!" continued the Chevalier, shaking the stick at Denot, upon whose arm the strong hand of the sergeant, who had returned to the room, was now laid heavily.

"I will choke the brat as I would an adder," said Denot, attempting to shake off the sergeant's hand. "There, take the dagger," and he dropped it on the ground, and rushing at the boy, got inside the swing of his stick, and made a grasp at his throat. Arthur, however, was too quick for him, and pushing away his hand, fastened his own arms round his adversary. They were now close locked in each other's embrace, and kicking, plunging, and striving, each did his best to throw the other to the ground.

"Oh! Sir, kind Sir, for mercy's sake separate them!" said Agatha, appealing to Santerre; "he is but a boy, a child, and that wretched man is mad. He'll murder the boy before your eyes, if you do not separate them."

"He won't find it so easy though," said the Chevalier, panting, and out of breath; but still holding his own, and, indeed, more than his own; for he had fixed his left hand in Denot's hair, and was pulling his head backwards with such force, that he nearly broke his neck.

"I think the young one has the best of it," said Santerre; "but come, citizen Denot, your loves and your quarrels are troublesome to us; we have other work to attend to. Get up, man, get up, I tell you."

Denot, by his superior weight and strength, had succeeded in getting the Chevalier to the ground, but Arthur still kept his hold in his hair, and though Adolphe was on the top of his foe, he did not find it very easy to get up.

"Get up, I say," said Santerre. "You'll gain nothing by wrestling with that fellow; he's more than a match for you. Well, Captain, what's the matter?"

The room in which the party had passed the night looked out into the garden at the back of the house. The front room communicated with this by folding-doors, which during the night had been closed. These doors were now violently thrown open, and one of the officers, followed by about a dozen men, rushed into the room.

"The road is crowded with men," said the officer; "thousands of these brigands are on us. The château will be surrounded in five minutes."

"H—— and the d——," said Santerre between his teeth. "This comes of playing the fool here," and he hurried out of the room in company with the officer.

"Hurrah!" said the Chevalier, jumping to his feet. "I knew they'd be here soon—I knew they'd be here soon," and running to Agatha's side he caught hold of her hand, and covered it with kisses.

Denot also arose. He had also heard the officer say that the peasants were coming on them, and he felt that if he were taken, he could expect no mercy from those who had so lately been his friends. He did not, however, attempt to fly, but he stood still on the spot where he got up, and after wiping his hot brow with his handkerchief, he said slowly and mournfully—"Agatha Larochejaquelin, you now see to what your conduct has reduced me; and with my last breath I tell you that I owe my disgrace, my misery, and my death—ay, and the loss of my eternal soul, to you, and to you only. Ay, shudder and shake, thou lovely monster of cruelty. Shake and grieve with remorse and fear. You may well do so. My living form shall trouble you no more, but dead and dying I will be with you till the last trump sounds on the fearful day of judgment."

Agatha did not answer him. She felt assured that he was mad, and she only pitied him. She had now too reason to hope that she and her father, and their whole household, would be relieved from their horrible position, and she no longer felt anything like anger against the unfortunate wretch whom uncontrolled passions had absolutely maddened. Arthur, in his anxiety to see what was going forward, was about to leave the room, but Agatha laid her hand upon his arm to detain him, merely looking towards Denot as she did so.

"And do you think," said Denot, "that puny boy could really stop my way, if I chose to put out my right hand against him. Boy, I despise and disregard you! would before I die that it might be allowed me to measure arms with any man, who would dare to say that he would advocate your cause!"

"Beware the switch, traitor—beware the switch!" repeated the Chevalier.

"Be quiet, Arthur, do not anger him," whispered Agatha. "It is not generous, you know, to insult a fallen foe."

"There are no terms to be kept with a traitor, Agatha. If we get the better of this, Santerre, as I am sure we shall now, you shall see that I know how to treat a generous foe generously."

When Santerre reached the front of the house, he at once saw that any attempt on his part to oppose the crowd of armed peasants who were now close upon him, would be futile. The only mode of escape which appeared to him at all practicable, was to attempt to ride through them. He gave the command "to horse," and got so far himself as to mount into his saddle; but it was of no use, he was surrounded by a crowd of peasants before he got to the gate, and he soon found himself on foot again, and unarmed. Some ten or twenty of his men, who were ready to jump into the saddle at the moment when they were first aware of the approach of the royalists, escaped, but the remainder in a few minutes found themselves prisoners in the château.

The peasants were headed by Father Jerome, the priest of St. Laud, and it was he who first mounted the steps leading up to the front door of the house. "Thank God," said he, speaking more to himself than to those around him. "Thank God!" and he stood up against the pedestal of one of the lions, the heavy wooden crucifix which he had carried in his hand as he marched, or rather ran, to the succour of his friends at Durbellière; and then he took off his cap, and with the sleeve of his dusty grey coat he wiped the perspiration from off his brow. "And the Marquis and Mademoiselle are unhurt? Thank God—thank God! we were just in time, but we had a smart run for it."

Chapeau had already dived into the kitchen through the window, and had learnt that at any rate the republicans had as yet shed no blood.

"And how did the Marquis bear it, Momont?" said he. "It was enough to kill the old gentleman."

"'Why, yes," said Momont. "We had to bear a good deal, but we did bear it manfully and well. We were all led out to be shot, you know."

"What, the Marquis and Mademoiselle and all?" said Chapeau.

"No, not the Marquis and Mademoiselle; they were to be beheaded after us, but the rest of us were all taken out—the muskets loaded—the men to shoot us all in a line."

"Oh! Chapeau, it was so awfully dreadful," said the cook. "If I live a thousand years I shall never get over this night."

"Oh, yes! most dreadfully awful," said the laundress. "I was carried in from the spot, and have not been able to move a limb since. I doubt I never shall put a foot to the ground again."

"The muskets were to their shoulders," continued Momont. "We heard them cocked: each man took deliberate aim; the women here were screeching and screaming."

"Of course we were," said the confidential maid. "Hadn't we good cause to scream, waiting to be killed every minute. I'm sure I wonder I ever came to my senses again. I declare when they came to pick me up, I thought it was all over, and that I'd been shot already."

"Well, I don't think anybody heard me scream," said Momont: "but there's a difference I know between a man and a woman. 'It's all for my

King and my master,' said I to myself. Besides a man can die but once, and it's a great thing to die honourably." The old man turned round to receive the approbation, which he considered was due to the sentiment he had expressed, and found that Chapeau was gone. The kitchen, however, was filled with peasants, and in them Momont found ready listeners and warm admirers.

Both Chapeau and the priest had spent the greater portion of the night in collecting what they considered would be a sufficient number of men to enable them to attack, with any chance of success, the republican soldiers who had taken possession of Durbellière. They had neither of them the slightest idea what amount of force had been brought against the château, and, consequently, wasted much time in procuring many more men than were necessary for the purpose. The three hundred, who were immediately got together on the sounding of the tocsin in the village of Echanbroignes, would have been sufficient to have done the work without further assistance, for they were all well armed, and, by this time, tolerably well trained in the use of their arms.

There was ten times more confusion now in the château, than there had been during the night: every room and passage was crowded with peasants, who took up their positions there under the plea of guarding their prisoners, and with the girls and women of the neighbourhood who flocked to that place, as soon as they heard that the horrible blues were all prisoners, and that the Marquis and Mademoiselle were once more at liberty. Agatha's troubles were by no means ended. Provisions of some kind were to be procured for the friends who had come so far and done so much to relieve them; and she had no one on whom she could depend to assist her in procuring them: the servants all considered themselves utterly unfitted for anything, except talking of the events of the evening; and though every one was burning with affection and zeal for Monseigneur and Mademoiselle, no one appeared willing to make himself useful.

The reaction on his feelings was too much for the poor Marquis. During the long evening and night, in which he had been a prisoner and looking forward to nothing but death; in which he had sat beside his fondly-loved daughter, whose fate he feared would be so much more horrible than death itself, he had patiently and manfully born his sufferings; he had even displayed a spirit for which few gave him credit, who were accustomed to his gentle temper and mild manners; but the unexpected recovery of his own and his daughter's liberty upset him entirely. As soon as he had pressed Father Jerome's hand, and thanked Chapeau fur what he had done, he begged that he might be carried off to his bed, and left there quietly till the return of his son, for whom, he was told, a messenger had been sent.

Santerre and Denot were both kept under a strong guard in the saloon in which they had passed the night; and there the priest, Chapeau, and the young Chevalier passed the greater part of the day, anxiously waiting the arrival of Henri Larochejaquelin.

"I never liked that man," said the priest, whispering to Arthur and Chapeau, for the latter, from his exertion and zeal was looked upon rather as an officer in the royalist army, than as a servant. "I never liked Adolphe Denot, but I could never say why. The tone of his voice was disagreeable to me, and the expression of his features aroused in me both dislike and distrust. It is not long since M. Henri rebuked me for being hard on him, and judging him harshly; and I was angry with myself for having done so. I knew, however, there was something wrong within him. He has turned out to be as base a creature as ever trod the earth."

"It will be a desperate blow to M. Henri," said Chapeau, "for he loved him as though he were his brother."

"I will be his brother now," said Arthur; "he shall love me in his place."

"Ah! M. Arthur," said Chapeau, "his heart is large enough to love us both; but when he hears how nobly you behaved last night, how you stood by Mademoiselle Agatha, and protected her, you will be his real brother indeed."

The little Chevalier's heart rose high within him, as he attempted to speak slightingly of his own services. "Oh!" said he, "I couldn't do much, you know, for I had only a stick; but of course we red scarfs will always stick to each other. Denot, you know, never was a red scarf Well, thank heaven for that; but I tell you what, Father Jerome, that Santerre is not such a bad fellow; and so I shall tell Henri; he is not a bad fellow at all, and he scorns Denot as he deserves to be scorned."

CHAPTER XI
ANNOT STEIN

It will be remembered that the party escaping from the Château of Clisson met Jean Stein, when they had come within four or five leagues of Durbellière. He had been sent from Echanbroignes, by Chapeau, to tell Henri what had happened, to assure him that every possible effort would be made to rescue his father and sister from the republicans, and if possible to save the château, and to beg him to return home as speedily as he possibly could. Jean was spared the greatest portion of his journey, and having told his tale, added that perhaps "Messieurs would not think it prudent to take the ladies with them to Durbellière just at present."

"Oh heavens! what are we to do?" said Madame de Lescure; "we are running from one hostile army into the middle of another. Poor Agatha! my poor Agatha! what will become of her?"

"Had we not better send them to Chatillon?" said Henri, speaking to de Lescure. "They will, at any rate, be safe there for a time."

"We won't be sent any where—indeed we won't—will we, Marie?" said Madame de Lescure. "Pray, Charles, pray do not send us away. Let us go where you go. It cannot be worse for us than it is for you."

"You cannot go to the château, dearest, when we have every reason to suppose it is in the hands of the republicans, and more than probably burnt to the ground by this time."

"Oh! don't send me back to Chatillon," said Marie; "it would be hours and hours before we should hear what happens to you, and what has happened to Agatha."

"If the ladies wouldn't think ill of going to Echanbroignes," said Jean Stein, "they would be safe there, and near at hand to learn all as it goes on at Durbellière. I am sure father and Annot would do their best to make the ladies comfortable, as long as they might be pleased to stay there."

After considerable discussion this plan was adopted. The party travelled on together, till the roads to Durbellière and Echanbroignes separated; and then, with many charges, the two ladies were entrusted to the care of the smith's son.

"We will come to you, or send to you the moment we are able," said de Lescure, "whether our news be good or bad. I trust we shall find them safe, and that we shall all be together tomorrow at Durbellière."

Marie and Madame de Lescure reached the village safely late in the evening, and found no one in the smith's house but Annot. Even Michael Stein himself had been moved by hearing that the republicans were absolutely in possession of the château, and, old as he was, he had made his way over to Durbellière, and had not yet returned. Annot, however, received them with good news; she had heard different messages from the château during the day, and was able to tell them not only that the Marquis, Agatha, and the house were safe, but that the republican soldiers were all prisoners, and that Santerre—that object of horror to many Vendean royalists, had himself been captured by the strong hand and bold heart of Jacques Chapeau.

Neither of the ladies knew Annot Stein, or had even heard of her; but Annot, though at present she was rather doleful, was not long in making herself known to them, and explaining to them her own particular connexion with the château.

She made up her own bed for one of them, and her father's for the other. They were not, she said, such as ladies like them were accustomed to sleep on, but the sheets were clean, and perhaps for one night they would excuse the want of better accommodation. Madame de Lescure and Marie declared that they were only too happy in being able to rest quietly, with the knowledge that their friends were in safety. Poor ladies! they were destined before long to encounter worse hardships than Annot Stein's little bed, and frugal supper.

"But, Madame," said Annot, as she sat demurely on the corner of her chair, "this Santerre is not the sort of man at all we all took him to be. Peter was over here, though he has gone back again now, and Peter says he is quite a good fellow in his way."

"What, Santerre!" said Marie, shuddering. "Oh! he is a most horrid monster! It was he that led out our dear sainted King to be murdered; it was he that urged on the furious mob to spill so much blood. They say that in all Paris there is not a greater wretch than this Santerre."

"I don't know, Mademoiselle," said Annot, "but he certainly wasn't so bad last night, for he might have killed them all had he chosen: and instead of that he didn't kill any one, or let any of his party kill them either, only he frightened poor old Momont nearly to death."

"God may have softened his heart," said Madame de Lescure; "if he has really spared our friends, we will not speak ill of him."

"If he has done so," said Marie, "he will have his reward; for I am sure Charles and Henri will spare him now that he is in their power."

"That's just what the people say," said Annot; "they say that it's M. Henri's turn to be generous now, and that they're sure he won't hurt a hair of this Santerre. Only they're determined on one thing—and it was all Chapeau and Father Jerome could do to stop them till M. Henri came home—they are determined to hang that horrid wretch Denot, the monster! I shouldn't wonder if he were swinging by this time."

"And is it really true," said Madame de Lescure, "that it was M. Denot who led the republicans to Durbellière?"

"Oh! that's a positive fact," said Annot, "there's no doubt on earth about that; and behaved most brutally to Mademoiselle Agatha. He would have killed her with his own hand, before her father, only M. Santerre wouldn't let him. He had his dagger out and all, and M. Santerre took it from him with his own hand, and wouldn't let him speak another word. Oh! indeed, ladies, M. Santerre is not half so bad as he looks to be."

"People say that the father of evil himself is painted blacker than he really is," said Marie.

"I don't know about that, Mademoiselle, and I didn't hear that this Santerre was painted black at all; and if he were so, I think Peter would have told me. But then, ladies, the little Chevalier Mondyon came in in the middle. It was he that sent Chapeau over here to bring the red scarfs to the rescue. He is a little darling, is the Chevalier. I suppose you know him, Mademoiselle?"

"Indeed I do, Annot, and love him dearly; he is an old sweetheart of mine."

"He's too young to have a sweetheart yet, Mademoiselle; but you'll see some of the ladies will be quarrelling for him yet, when he's a year or two older. Well, after sending Jacques over here, he went back as bold as possible into the middle of the republicans, before Santerre and all. M. Denot was at his worst then. He had hold of Mademoiselle Agatha, and was dragging her away from the Marquis, in spite of Santerre and the whole of them, when the Chevalier raises his stick, and strikes him across the face. I warrant you he let go Mademoiselle's hand when he felt the sharp stick come across his eyes."

"It must have been a horrid sight for Agatha," said Madame de Lescure.

"Oh! indeed it was, Madame. Only fancy that traitor Denot going on in that way, right before her eyes all night, and no one to protect her but the little Chevalier; for when it got late M. Santerre threw himself on the floor, and slept and snored like a hog. They say it was all for love, Mademoiselle. They say this Denot was greatly in love with Mademoiselle Agatha, and that she wouldn't look at him. Is it true, she was so very scornful to him?"

"She was never scornful to any one," said Marie; "but if he ever asked her for her love, I have no doubt she told him that she could not give it to him."

"That's just what they say; and that then he asked her more and more, and went down on his knees to her, and prayed her just as much as to look at him; and kissed her feet, and cried dreadfully; and that all she did was to turn aside her face, and bid him rise and leave her."

"What would you have had her say, Annot, if she felt that she could not love him?"

"Oh! I'm not presuming to find fault with her, Mademoiselle; heaven forbid! Of course, if she couldn't love him, she could do nothing but refuse him. But, heigho! it's a very dreadful thing to think of that a nice young man like him—for I'm told that this Denot was a very nice young man—should be so bewildered by love as he has been."

"Love couldn't make a man a traitor," said Marie, "nor yet a coward."

"I don't know, Mademoiselle, love is a very fearful thing when it doesn't go right. Perhaps love never made you feel so angry that you'd like to eat your lover's heart?"

"Gracious goodness, no," said Marie; "why, Annot, where did you get such a horrid idea as that?"

"Ah! Mademoiselle, your lover's one in a hundred! So handsome, so noble, so good, so grand, so amiable, so everything that a young lady could wish to dream about: one, too, that never has vagaries and jealousies, and nasty little aggravating ways. Oh! Mademoiselle, I look upon you as the happiest young lady in the world.

"What on earth, Annot, do you know about my lover, or how on earth can you know that I have a lover at all? Why, child, I and my cousin Agatha are both going to be nuns at St. Laurent."

"The blessed Virgin forbid it," said Annot. "Not but what Mademoiselle Agatha would look beautiful as a nun. She has the pale face, and the long straight nose, and the calm melancholy eyes, just as a nun ought to have; but then she should join the Carmelite ladies at the rich convent of our Blessed

Lady at St. Maxent, where they all wear beautiful white dresses and white hoods, and have borders to their veils, and look so beautiful that there need hardly be any change in them when they go to heaven; and not become one of those dusty-musty black sisters of mercy at St. Laurent."

"That's your idea of a nun, is it?" said Madame de Lescure.

"I'm sure, Madame, I don't know why any girl should try to make herself look ugly, if God has made her as beautiful as Mademoiselle Agatha."

"And you think then Mademoiselle de Lescure is not fit for a nun at all?"

"Oh, Madame, we all know she is going to be married immediately to the finest, handsomest, most noble young nobleman in all Poitou. Oh! I'd give all the world to have such a lover as M. Henri just for ten minutes, to see him once kneeling at my feet."

"For ten minutes," said Marie. "What good would that do you? that would only make you unhappy when the ten minutes were gone and past."

"Besides, what would you say to him in that short time?" said Madame de Lescure.

"Say to him! I don't know what I'd say to him. I don't think I'd say one word, but I'd give him such a look, so full of affection and gratitude, and admiration, and—and—and downright real true love; that, if he had any heart in him at all, I don't think he'd be so base as to go away from me when the ten minutes were over."

"That's what you call borrowing a lover for ten minutes, is it?" said Marie; "and if, as you say, this young gentleman is my property, what am I to do for a lover the while?"

"I was only wishing, Mademoiselle, and you know there's no harm in wishing. Besides, the finest lady in the world couldn't rob you of your lover, let alone a poor girl like me. He is so true, and so noble, and so good."

"And have not you a lover of your own, Annot?"

"Oh, indeed I have, and a very good one. For all my talking in that way, I was never badly off for lovers, and now I've chosen one for good and all; and I love him dearly, Madame; dote on him, and so does he on me, but for all that there was a time when I really would have eaten his heart, if I could have got at it."

"But that was before you had accepted each other."

"Not at all, Mademoiselle; not long since. I loved then as dearly as I do now, but he let me walk home by myself three long leagues without speaking a word to me, and all because I said that a man in a picture had fine whiskers."

"A man in a picture! why this lover of yours must be a very jealous man, or else he must be very badly off for whiskers himself?"

"No he's not, Mademoiselle; he's as nice a pair as you'd wish to see; that is, begging your pardon, as nice a pair as I'd wish to see; and he's not a jealous man either about other things."

"And when do you mean to marry him, Annot?"

"Oh, Mademoiselle, we are only waiting for you."

"Waiting for me, child! What on earth do you mean? who told you I was going to be married at all?"

It was no wonder that Marie should be astonished at finding her wedding so confidently spoken of by a stranger in Echanbroignes, considering that it was not yet twenty-four hours since Henri had declared his love for her at Clisson.

"But you are going to be married to M. Henri, are you not, Mademoiselle?"

"Who told you all this? how is it you come to know so much about this young lady and M. Henri?" said Madame de Lescure.

"Why, Jacques Chapeau told me. My own husband, that is, as is to be."

"Oh! that explains the mystery," said Marie; "and so Chapeau is your lover is he? Chapeau is the man who couldn't bear the mention of the fine pair of whiskers you saw in the picture? and did he tell you that his master was going to be married immediately?" and Marie blushed as she asked the question.

"Indeed he did, Mademoiselle, and he said besides—"

"Well, what did he say besides?"

"Why, I hardly like to say now, Mademoiselle; it will look like asking a favour when I thought you could not well refuse it; and perhaps Jacques was wrong to say anything at all about it."

Marie, however, was not long in inducing Annot to reveal to her Chapeau's little plan of taking his own wife over to Durbellière to wait upon his master's wife, and she, moreover, promised that, as far as she herself was concerned, she would consent to the arrangement, if, which she expressly inserted, she should ever marry M. Larochejaquelin.

"But an't you engaged to him, Mademoiselle?"

"Well, Annot," answered she, "as you have told me so much, I don't mind telling you that I am. But it will be long, probably, before I am married, if ever I am. Men have other things to think of now than marriage, and, alas! women too. We must wait till the wars are over, Annot."

"But I thought the wars were over now, Mademoiselle. Haven't they got that Santerre prisoner up at Durbellière?"

"There's much, very much, I fear to do yet, and to suffer, before the wars will be really over," said Madame de Lescure. "Heaven help us, and guide us, and protect us! Come, Marie, let us go to rest, for I trust Charles will send for us early in the morning."

Annot gave such assistance to her two guests as they required, and was within her power, and then seating herself in her father's large arm chair in the kitchen, pondered over the misery of living in times when men were so busy fighting with their enemies, that they had not even leisure to get married.

"And what, after all, is the use of these wars?" said she to herself "What do they get by taking so many towns, and getting so many guns, and killing so many men? I don't know who's the better for it, but I know very well who's the worse. Why can't they let the blues alone; and the blues let them alone? I worked my poor fingers to the bone making a white flag before they went to Saumur, and all they did was to leave it in the streets of Nantes. There's not so much as a bottle of beer, and hardly a bushel of flour left in Echanbroignes. There's the poor dear lovely Cathelineau dead and gone. There's M. Henri engaged to the girl of his heart, and he can't so much as stay a day from fighting to get himself married; and there's Jacques just as bad. If Jacques cares a bit for me, he must take himself off, and me with him, to some place where there's not quite so much fighting, or else I'll be quit of him and go without him. I've no idea of living in a place where girls are not, to be married till the wars are over. Wars, wars, wars; I'm sick of the wars with all my heart."

CHAPTER XII
SENTENCE OF DEATH

After parting with their companion, de Lescure and Henri were not long in reaching Durbellière; and on the road thither they also learnt that Santerre, and upwards of a hundred blue horsemen, were prisoners in the château, or in the barns, out-houses, or stables belonging to it; and that the whole place was crowded with peasants, guarding their captives. As they entered the château gates, they met Chapeau, who was at the bottom of the steps, waiting for them; and Henri immediately asked after his father.

"Monseigneur is much fatigued," said Chapeau, "but apparently well; he is, however, still in bed."

"And my sister?" said Henri.

"Mademoiselle has of course been much fatigued, but she is well; she is with your father, M. Henri."

"And tell me, Chapeau, is it true, is it really true that M. Denot brought the blues here, and that since he has been here he has treated my sister in the manner they describe?"

"It is true as gospel, M. Henri. I knew that this would be the worst of the whole affair to you. I knew you would sooner the château should have been burnt than have heard this. We are only waiting for you and M. de Lescure, to hang him as a traitor from the big chestnut out on the road-side. You might have seen as you came in, that they have the ropes and everything ready."

Henri shuddered as he followed his cousin into the house. The steps were crowded with his own followers, who warmly welcomed him, and congratulated him on the safety of his father, his sister, and his property; but he said very little to them; he was thinking of the friend whom he had loved so well, who had so vilely disgraced himself, and whose life he now feared he should be unable to save.

"Where is he?" said he to Chapeau.

"Who—Monseigneur?"

"No—M. Denot."

"He is in the great salon, with Santerre, and Father Jerome, and the Chevalier, and three or four of the lads from Echanbroignes."

"Charles," said he, as he reached the door of the salon, "do you go in. You are better able to say what should be said, and to do what must be done, than I am. I will go up to my father. But, Charles," and he spoke into his ear, so that no one else should hear him, "save his life—for my sake, save his life. He is mad, and does not know what he has been doing." De Lescure pressed his cousin's hand, and as Henri ran up stairs to his father, he entered the room, where the party abovementioned were sitting.

The occupants of the room certainly formed a very remarkable group. The first person whom de Lescure saw was Adolphe Denot; he was seated in a large arm-chair, placed against the wall immediately opposite the door, and between the stove and the folding-doors which opened into the other room. His legs were stretched out to their full length before him his hands were clasped together between his legs; his head was bent down, so that his chin rested on his breast; he was scowling awfully, his eyebrows nearly met above his eyes, and he continued constantly curling and twisting his lips, sometimes shewing his teeth, and sometimes completely covering his under with his upper lip. He had sat twelve hours, since Agatha had left the room in the morning, without speaking a word, or once changing his position. He had refused food when it had been brought to him, with an indignant shake of the head; and when Santerre had once half jocularly told him to keep up his spirits, and prove himself a man, he had uttered a horrible sound, which he had meant for a laugh of derision, such as is sometimes heard to proceed from dark-haired, diabolical, provincial tragedians.

There were three men from Echanbroignes in the room, distinguished by the notable red scarf, acting as guards, to prevent the escape of the prisoners; but as the two objects of their care during the whole day had made no attempt at escaping, the guards had by degrees laid aside the eager watchfulness with which they had at first expressed their readiness to pounce upon their captives, should they by any motion have betrayed an intention to leave their seats, and were now resting on three chairs in a row, each man having his musket between his legs, and looking as though they were peculiarly tired of their long inactive services. Santerre and Father Jerome were seated together on a sofa, and the Chevalier occupied a chair on the other side of a table on which the prisoner and the priest were leaning. When Santerre found that he and his men were in the hands of the royalist peasants, he at first rather lost both his temper and his presence of mind. He saw at once that resistance was out of the question, and that there was very little chance that he would be able to escape; he began to accuse himself of rashness in having accepted from the Convention the very disagreeable commission which had brought him into his present plight, and to wish that he was once more among his legitimate adherents in the Quartier St. Antoine. He soon, however, regained his equanimity. Those whom he had in his rough manner treated well, returned the compliment; and he perceived that, though he would probably be kept a prisoner, his life would not be in danger, and that the royalists were not inclined to treat him either with insult or severity.

He by degrees got into conversation with the Chevalier; and before the day was over, even Father Jerome, much as he abhorred a republican, and especially a leader of republicans, and an infidel, as he presumed Santerre to be, forgot his disgust, and chatted freely with the captive Commissioner. The three dined together in the afternoon, and when de Lescure entered the room, wine and glasses were still on the table. A crowd of the royalist peasants followed de Lescure to the door of the salon, and would have entered it with him, had not Chapeau, with much difficulty, restrained them. They were most anxious to hear sentence pronounced on the traitor, who had betrayed their cause, and insulted the sister of their favourite leader; and could not understand why the punishment, which he had so richly merited, should be delayed. All that Chapeau and Father Jerome had ventured to ask of them was to wait till Henri himself should arrive; and now, that he had come, they conceived that judgment should at once be passed, and sentence of death immediately executed.

When de Lescure entered the room, they all, except Denot, rose from their chairs; the three guards stood up, and shouldered their muskets, the Chevalier ran up to him to shake hands with him, and Father Jerome also came out into the middle of the room to meet him. He looked first at Denot, who kept his eyes steadily fixed on the ground; and then at Santerre, whom he had never, to his knowledge, seen before. Santerre, however, knew him, for he immediately called him by his name.

"My soldiers have met with a reverse, General de Lescure," said he, "which has thrown me and them into the power of your friends. I take the earliest opportunity of thanking you for the kind treatment we have received."

"If, at some future time, when our soldiers may be in your power, you will remember it; the Marquis de Larochejaquelin will feel himself amply repaid for such attention as he has been able to shew you," said de Lescure.

"You know we were in General Santerre's power last night," said the Chevalier; "and he could have shot us all had he pleased it; indeed we all expected it, when the blues came upon us."

"They shall not find that we will be less merciful, Arthur," said de Lescure. "General Santerre knows that the Vendean royalists have never disgraced themselves by shedding the blood of the prisoners whom the chance of war may have thrown into their hands. He knows that they can be brave without being cruel. I grieve to say that the republicans have hitherto not often allowed us to repay mercy with mercy. We shall now be glad to take advantage of the opportunity of doing so."

"What will you do with him, M. de Lescure," said Father Jerome in a whisper, pointing to Denot. "I never before saw the people greedy for blood; but now they declare that no mercy should be shown to a traitor."

"We must teach them, Father Jerome, that it is God's will that those who wish to be pardoned themselves must pardon others. You have taught them lessons more difficult to learn than this; and I do not doubt that in this, as in other things, they will obey their priest." And as he spoke de Lescure laid his hand on the Curé's shoulder.

"You won't hang him then?" whispered the Chevalier.

"You wouldn't have me do so, would you, Arthur?"

"Who—I?" said the boy. "No—that is, I don't know. I wouldn't like to have to say that anybody should be hung; but if anybody ever did deserve it, he does."

"And you, Father Jerome?" said de Lescure, "you agree with me? You would not have us sully our pure cause with a cold-blooded execution?"

The three were now standing at an open window, looking into the garden. Their backs were turned to Santerre and Denot, and they were speaking in low whispers; but nevertheless Denot either guessed or overheard that he was the subject of their conversation. The priest did not immediately answer de Lescure's appeal. In his heart he thought that the circumstances not only justified, but demanded the traitor's death; but, remembering his profession, and the lessons of mercy it was his chief business to teach, he hesitated to be the first to say that he thought the young man should be doomed.

"Well, Father Jerome," said de Lescure, looking into the priest's face, "surely you have no difficulty in answering me?"

The Curé was saved the necessity of answering the appeal; for while he was still balancing between what he thought to be his duty, and that which was certainly his inclination, Denot himself interrupted the whisperers.

"M. de Lescure," said he, in the deep, hoarse, would-be solemn voice, which he now always affected to use. De Lescure turned quickly round, and so did his companions. The words of a man who thinks that he is almost immediately about to die are always interesting.

"If you are talking about me," said the unfortunate wretch, "pray spare yourself the trouble. I neither ask, nor wish for any mercy at your hands. I am ready to die."

As de Lescure looked at him, and observed the alteration which a few weeks had made in his appearance—his sunken, sallow cheeks; his wild and bloodshot eyes; his ragged, uncombed hair, and soiled garments—as he thought of his own recent intimacy with him—as he remembered how often he had played with him as a child, and associated with him as a man—that till a few days since he had been the bosom friend of his own more than brother, Henri Larochejaquelin, the tears rushed to his eyes and down his cheeks. In that moment the scene in the council-room at Saumur came to his mind, and he remembered that there he had rebuked Adolphe Denot for his false ambition, and had probably been the means of driving him to the horrid crime which he had committed. Though he knew that the traitor's iniquity admitted of no excuse, he sympathized with the sufferings which had brought him to his present condition. He turned away his head, as the tears rolled down his cheeks, and felt that he was unable to speak to the miserable man.

Had de Lescure upbraided him, Denot's spirit, affected and unreal as it was, would have enabled him to endure it without flinching. He would have answered the anger of his former friend with bombast, and might very probably have mustered courage enough to support the same character till they led him out to death. But de Lescure's tears affected him. He felt that he was pitied; and though his pride revolted against the commiseration of those whom he had injured, his heart was touched, and his voice faltered, as he again declared that he desired no mercy, and that he was ready to die.

"Ready to die!" said the Curé, "and with such a weight of sin upon your conscience; ready to be hurried before the eternal judgment seat, without having acknowledged, even in your own heart, the iniquity of your transgressions!"

"That, Sir, is my concern," said Denot. "I knew the dangers of the task before I undertook it, and I can bear the penalties of failure without flinching. I fear them not, either in this world or in any other world to come."

De Lescure, overcome with distress, paced up and down the room till Chapeau entered it, and whispered to him, that the peasants outside were anxious to know what next they were to do, and that they were clamorous for Denot's execution. "They are determined to hang him," continued Chapeau, who had induced de Lescure to leave the room, and was now speaking to him in the hall. "They say that you and M. Henri may do what you please about Santerre and the soldiers, but that Adolphe Denot has betrayed the cause, insulted Mademoiselle, and proved himself unfit to live; and that they will not leave the château as long as a breath of life remains in his body."

"And you, Chapeau, what did you say to them in reply?"

"Oh, M. de Lescure, of course I said that that must be as you and M. Henri pleased."

"Well, Chapeau, now go and tell them this," said de Lescure: "tell them that we will not consent that this poor wretch shall be killed, and that his miserable life has already been granted to him. Tell them also, that if they choose to forget their duty, their obedience, and their oaths, and attempt to seize Denot's person, neither I nor M. Henri will ever again accompany them to battle, and that they shall not lay a hand upon him till they have passed over our bodies. Do you understand?"

Chapeau said that he did understand, and with a somewhat melancholy face, he returned to the noisy crowd, who were waiting for their victim in the front of the house. "Well, Jacques," said one of them, an elderly man, who had for the time taken upon himself the duties of a leader among them, and who was most loud in demanding that sentence should be passed upon Denot. "We are ready, and the rope is ready, and the gallows is ready, and we are only waiting for the traitor. We don't want to hurry M. Henri or M. de Lescure, but we hope they will not keep us waiting much longer."

"You need not wait any longer," said Chapeau, "for Adolphe Denot is not to be hung at all. M. de Lescure has pardoned him. Yes, my friends, you will be spared an unpleasant job, and the rope and the tree will not be contaminated."

"Pardoned him—pardoned Adolphe Denot—pardoned the traitor who brought Santerre and the republicans to Durbellière—pardoned the wretch who so grossly insulted Mademoiselle Agatha, and nearly killed M. le Marquis," cried one after another immediately round the door. "If we pardon him, there will be an end of honesty and good faith. We will pardon our enemies, because M. de Lescure asks us. We will willingly pardon this Santerre and all his men. We will pardon everything and anybody, if M. Henri or M de Lescure asks it, except treason, and except a traitor. Go in, Jacques, and say that we will never consent to forgive the wretch who insulted Mademoiselle Larochejaquelin. By all that is sacred we will hang him!"

"If you do, my friends," answered Chapeau, "you must kill M. de Lescure first, for he will defend him with his own body and his own sword."

Chapeau again returned to the house, and left the peasants outside, loudly murmuring. Hitherto they had passively obeyed their leaders. They had gone from one scene of action to another. They had taken towns and conquered armies, and abstained not only from slaughter, but even from plunder, at the mere request of those whom they had selected as their own Generals; now, for the first time they shewed a determination to disobey. The offence of which their victim had been guilty, was in their eyes unpardonable. They were freely giving all—their little property, their children, their blood, for their church and King. They knew that they were themselves faithful and obedient to their leaders, and they could not bring themselves to forgive one whom they had trusted, and who had deceived them.

Chapeau returned to the house, but he did not go back to M. de Lescure. He went upstairs to his master, and found him alone with his sister, and explained to them what was going on before the front-door.

"They will never go away, Mademoiselle, as long as the breath is in the man's body. They are angry now, and they care for no one, not even for M. Henri himself; and it's no wonder for them to be angry. He that was so trusted, and so loved; one of the family as much as yourself, M. Henri. Why, if I were to turn traitor, and go over to the republicans, it could hardly be worse. If ever I did, I should expect them to pinch me to pieces with hot tweezers, let alone hanging."

"I will go down to them," said M. Henri.

"It will be no use," said Chapeau, "they will not listen to you."

"I will try them at any rate, for they have never yet disobeyed me. I know they love me, and I will ask for Adolphe's life as a favour to myself: if they persist in their cruelty, if they do kill him, I will lay down my sword, and never again raise it in La Vendée."

"If it were put off for a week, or a day, M. Henri, so that they could get cool; if you could just consent to his being hung, but say that he was to have four-and-twenty hours to prepare himself, and then at the end of that time they wouldn't care about it: mightn't that do? Wouldn't that be the best plan, Mademoiselle?"

"No," said Henri. "I will not stoop to tell them a falsehood; nor if I did so, would they ever believe me again." And he walked towards the passage, intending to go down to the front-door.

"Stop, Henri, stop a moment!" said Agatha, "I will go down to them. I will speak to them. They are not accustomed to hear me speak to them in numbers, as they are to you, and that of itself will make them inclined to listen to me. I will beg them to spare the unfortunate man, and I think they will not refuse me."

She got up and walked to the door, and her brother did not attempt to stop her.

"Let me go alone, Henri," said she. "You may, at any rate, be sure that they will not hurt me." And, without waiting for his reply, she descended the stairs, and walked into the hall. When Chapeau left them, the crowd were collected immediately in the front of the house and on the steps, but none of them had yet forced their way into the château; since he had gone upstairs, however, they had pushed open the door, and now filled the hall; although their accustomed respect for the persons and property of those above them, had still kept them from breaking into the room, in which they knew were M. de Lescure and Adolphe Denot. The foremost of them drew back when they saw Agatha come among them, and as she made her way to the front-door, they retreated before her, till she found herself standing on the top of the steps, and surrounded by what seemed to her a countless crowd of heads. There was a buzz of many voices among them, and she stood there silent before them a moment or two, till there should be such silence as would enable them to hear her.

Agatha Larochejaquelin had never looked more beautiful than she did at this time. Her face was more than ordinarily pale, for her life had lately been one of constant watching and deep anxiety; but hers was a countenance which looked even more lovely without than with its usual slight tinge of colour. Her beautiful dark-brown hair was braided close to her face, and fastened in a knot behind her head. She was dressed in a long white morning wrapper, which fell quite down over her feet, and added in appearance to her natural high stature. She seemed to the noisy peasants, as she stood there before them, sad-looking and sorrowful, but so supremely beautiful, to be like some goddess who had come direct from heaven to give them warning and encouragement. The hum of their voices soon dropped, and they stood as silent before her, as though no strong passion, no revenge and thirst for blood had induced them, but a moment before, all but to mutiny against the leaders who had led them so truly, and loved them so well.

"Friends, dear friends," she began in her sweet voice, low, but yet plainly audible to those whom she addressed; and then she paused a moment to think of the words she would use to them, and as she did so they cheered her loudly, and blessed her, and assured her, in their rough way, how delighted they were to have saved her and the Marquis from their enemies.

"Dear friends," she continued, "I have come to thank you for the readiness and kindness with which you have hurried to my protection—to tell you how grateful I and mine are for your affection, and at the same time to ask a favour from your hands."

"God bless you, Mademoiselle. We will do anything for Mademoiselle Agatha. We all know that Mademoiselle is an angel. We will do anything for her," said different voices in the crowd. "Anything but pardon the traitor who has insulted her," said the man who had been most prominent in demanding Denot's death. "Anything at all—anything, without exception. We will do anything we are asked, whatever it is, for Mademoiselle Agatha," said some of the younger men among the crowd, whom her beauty made more than ordinarily enthusiastic in her favour. "Mademoiselle will not sully her beautiful lips to ask the life of a traitor," said another. "We will do anything else; but Denot must die." "Yes, Denot must die," exclaimed others. "He shall die; he is not fit to live. When the traitor is hung, we will do anything, go anywhere, for Mademoiselle."

"Ah! friends," said she, "the favour I would ask of you is to spare the life of this miserable young man. Hear me, at any rate," she continued, for there was a murmur among the more resolute of Denot's enemies. "You will not refuse to hear what I say to you. You demand vengeance, you say, because he has betrayed your cause, and insulted me. If I can forgive the insult, if my brother can, surely you should do so too. Think, dear friends, what my misery must be, if on my account you shed the blood of this poor creature. You say he has betrayed the cause for which you are fighting. It is true, he has done so; but it is not only your cause which he has betrayed. Is it not my cause also? Is it not my brother's? Is it not M. de Lescure's? And if we can forgive him, should not you also do so too? He has lived in this house as though he were a child of my father's. You know that my brother has treated him as a brother. Supposing that you, any of you, had had a brother who has done as he has done, would you not still pray, in spite of his crimes, that he might be forgiven? I know you all love my brother. He deserves from you that you should love him well, for he has proved to you that he loves you. He—Henri Larochejaquelin—your own leader, begs you to forgive the crime of his adopted brother. Have we not sufficient weight with you—are we not near enough to your hearts, to obtain from you this boon?"

"We will, we will," shouted they; "we will forgive—no, we won't forgive him, but we'll let him go; only, Mademoiselle, let him go from this—

let him not show himself here any more. There, lads, there's an end of it. Give Momont back the rope. We will do nothing to displease M. Henri and Mademoiselle Agatha," and then they gave three cheers for the inhabitants of Durbellière; and Agatha, after thanking them for their kindness and their courtesy, returned into the house.

For some days after the attack and rescue, there was great confusion in the château of Durbellière. The peasants by degrees returned to their own homes, or went to Chatillon, at which place it was now intended to muster the whole armed royalist force which could be collected in La Vendée. Chatillon was in the very centre of the revolted district, and not above three leagues from Durbellière; and at this place the Vendean leaders had now determined to assemble, that they might come to some fixed plan, and organize their resistance to the Convention.

De Lescure and Henri together agreed to give Santerre his unconditional liberty. In the first place, they conceived it to be good policy to abandon the custody of a man whom, if kept a prisoner, they were sure the Republic would make a great effort to liberate; and who, if he ever again served against them at all, would, as they thought, be less inclined to exercise barbarity than any other man whom the Convention would be likely to send on the duty. Besides, Agatha and the Marquis really felt grateful to Santerre, for having shown a want of that demoniac cruelty with which they supposed him to have been imbued; and it was, therefore, resolved to escort him personally to the northern frontier of La Vendée, and there set him at liberty, but to detain his soldiers prisoners at Chatillon; and this was accordingly done.

They had much more difficulty in disposing of Denot. Had he been turned loose from the château, to go where he pleased, and do what he pleased, he would to a certainty have been killed by the peasantry. De Lescure asked Santerre to take charge of him, but this he refused to do, saying that he considered the young man was a disgrace to any party, or any person, who had aught to do with him, and that he would not undertake to be responsible for his safety.

Denot himself would neither say or do anything. Henri never saw him; but de Lescure had different interviews with him, and did all in his power to rouse him to some feeling as to the future; but all in vain. He usually refused to make any answer whatever, and when he did speak, he merely persisted in his declaration that he was willing to die, and that if he were left alive, he had no wish at all as to what should become of him. It was at last decided to send him to his own house at Fleury, with a strong caution to the servants there that their master was temporarily insane; and there to leave him to his chance. "When he finds himself alone, and disregarded," said de Lescure, "he will come to his senses, and probably emigrate: it is impossible for us now to do more for him. May God send that he may live to repent the great crime which he has attempted."

Now again everything was bustle and confusion at Durbellière. Arms and gunpowder were again collected. The men again used all their efforts in assembling the royalist troops, the women in preparing the different necessaries for the army. The united families were at Durbellière, and there was no longer any danger of their separation, for at Clisson not one stone was left standing upon another.